COWBOY BOOTS

BY SHANNON GARST

ILLUSTRATED BY CHARLES HARGENS

A

COWBOY BOOTS

ABINGDON-COKESBURY PRESS
NEW YORK & NASHVILLE

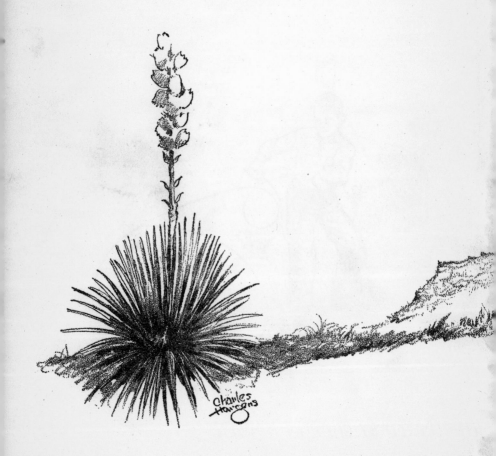

TO BARBARA JO

THE CHAPTERS

COWBOY BOOTS

At last Bob saw
a herd of cattle

1. Off to Adventure

BOB BENTON sat up, stared around, and blinked his brown eyes. Where was he? Why was he shut in this little place? Then he remembered. He was in a berth on the train, on his way to his Uncle John's cattle ranch in Wyoming to spend the summer. A pleasant sense of excitement came over him.

It was morning, and he must be in Wyoming. He peered out the window. Sure enough, the country looked quite different, yet for some reason he felt a bit disappointed. He didn't know exactly what it was he expected to see, but it wasn't this bleak, barren land. For miles the country stretched without a tree or a house in sight. Nothing but gray sagebrush and telegraph poles rushing by.

At last Bob saw a herd of cattle and he sighed with relief. He strained his eyes trying to catch sight of a galloping cowboy. Where there were cattle there must be cowboys, but there was none in sight. Still, he felt better. It was cowboy land, all right. Somewhere, not too far away, must be his uncle's Circle K Ranch.

There was a sound at the heavy curtains that shut his berth off from the aisle, and he heard the porter say, "You all'd better be gettin' up. We're due at Long Horn in half an hour."

Bob began scrambling into his clothes as if he had only five minutes instead of thirty. He took his toothbrush and comb and went swaying down the aisle to the washroom.

He hurried so much that he still had a little time to stand at the corridor window and watch the fence posts and telegraph poles rush by. Every time the train passed a herd of cattle, Bob's heart leaped with excitement. But still he saw no cowboys. The train whistled and began to slow down. He dashed up the aisle after the porter.

When the train stopped, Bob hurried down the steps onto the station platform. He looked about and felt slightly disappointed. Long Horn was just another unexciting looking town, much like the small towns he had passed through in Colorado. There were no cowboys whooping through the sleepy streets. Then he saw his uncle coming up. To Bob's disappointment he wore ordinary clothes, except for the wide hat that did look a bit cowboyish.

"Howdy, partner! Glad to see you." Uncle John gave

12

his nephew's hand a squeeze that made Bob wince. "I was really surprised that your father and mother let you come all the way out here from Chicago alone. And that they'd trust their only chick to an old bachelor for a whole summer!"

Bob laughed. "It took plenty of talk before they made up their minds," he admitted. "But Dad couldn't get away from the office this summer, and Mother thought it would do me good to be outdoors. Besides," he gave his uncle an eager look, "they know I want to be a cowboy."

"So you want to be a cowboy!" John Benton chuckled. "But right now, I reckon, you want to eat. So do I. Come along and we'll have some 'chuck' before we start out. It's a long trip to the Circle K."

John Benton picked up Bob's suitcase and started down the broad street. Bob had to stretch his legs to keep up. They entered a dingy restaurant and sat on high stools at the counter.

As they were waiting for their order, the door opened and in stalked a tall, lean man. Bob caught his breath sharply, for he knew instantly that here was a real cowboy. He wore high-heeled boots with clinking spurs and a green plaid shirt and orange neckerchief. A very wide hat was pushed to the back of his head. He did not wear chaps, but faded blue overalls with, low on his hips, a wide belt of carved and silver-studded leather.

"Howdy, Montana," John Benton called. "We didn't wait, because Bob, our new hand here, was hungry. Bob, this is Montana, the Circle K's foreman."

Bob nearly fell off his stool with excitement. Montana might have stepped squarely out of one of his dreams. He looked just as a cowboy should look. His face was handsome in a rugged, masculine sort of way. And there was something about his bearing that made Bob feel that here was a man always to be trusted and counted on.

"Howdy." Montana's hand reached over to give Bob's a strong grip. "I'm right glad you're going to be with us at the Circle K. Indeed I am."

Then turning to John Benton he said, "I shouldn't be surprised if we had the makings of a top hand here. Freckle-faced, red-headed boys generally make good top hands."

Bob did not know what a top hand was, but coming from Montana the words sounded good to him. His chest swelled, only to be deflated promptly by his uncle's words, "Bob's only twelve—a bit too young to be much help. But he can have plenty of fun on the ranch. That's what he's come here for."

"Oh, no!" Bob cried. "I want to be a real cowboy."

But his uncle and Montana had begun to talk about yearlings and two-year-olds and market conditions and hardly seemed to hear him.

14

As soon as they finished breakfast, the three of them went out to the car. Its open back was piled high with boxes of groceries.

Bob sat between Uncle John, who drove, and Montana. He looked at the rolling green hills with herds of cattle grazing on them. Every now and then he saw a low, comfortable looking ranch house with barns and other buildings clustered about it.

"Where are all the cowboys?" he asked.

"Oh, you'll see plenty of them when you get to the Circle K," his uncle answered.

The blue hills crept nearer. Finally the car jounced over the iron rails that formed a cattle guard leading into the ranch.

Montana noticed Bob's questioning look. "Livestock won't try to walk over those rails, because their feet would catch in the spaces between them," he explained. "But cars can cross, and no one has to get out and open the gate."

Over the gate Bob saw a big sign—CIRCLE K RANCH—painted in blue letters. Above the letters was a bleached steer skull with long horns.

Bob sat up straight and looked about. On one side of the road was an alfalfa field, purple with blossoms. On the other side were sandstone buttes shaped like ancient castles and battlements. That would be a fine place to play Indian, he thought, and he wondered if real Indians had ever had a battle fortress there.

Soon they drove up to a rambling house, nestled in a grove of cottonwoods. It was made of logs, and a screened porch ran across the front. Behind the house Bob saw barns, the bunkhouse, and outbuildings, and adjoining these a large, circular corral enclosed by upright poles. He heard the gurgle of a stream a short distance away. Then his eye caught sight of a number of saddles thrown over a fence.

"What a wonderful place!" he cried, and his brown eyes sparkled with delight.

A tan-and-white shepherd collie dog came bounding to meet the car. At his heels leaped a young antelope.

"Jumping Jimminy!" Bob exclaimed. "What's that?"

"This is Shep," said Uncle John, patting the collie's head. "I expect you two will be great pals. And this is our pet antelope. He hasn't a name yet. We'll let you give him one."

Bob patted the smooth head of the little animal while it butted him playfully.

"Jumping Jimminy!" he cried again. "This is going to be great. A dog and an antelope for pets! And—and I s'pose I'll have a horse to ride, and everything."

The last words blurted themselves out. Bob felt that it wasn't quite polite to be asking for a horse so soon,

16

*A dog and an antelope
for pets!*

but the subject had been at the top of his mind for so long that he could not keep the words back. He could hardly wait to get on one of the horses he saw in the big corral and go galloping across the green plain.

"Whoa now!" his uncle laughed. "Not so fast. Have you ever been on a horse?"

"No-o," Bob admitted. "Not yet. But I know I can ride. Of course I haven't any cowboy boots yet, but I'm sure my dad will send some soon."

He looked again at Montana's handsome, elaborately stitched boots. To him they stood for everything that was cowboyish, and his longing for cowboy boots of his own was so strong that it hurt.

"Well," his uncle said as he led the way into the house, "it takes a lot more than fancy clothes to make a cowboy. A lot more."

Bob remembered that his father had told him that very thing.

John Benton led the way into a large, cool room, cozy with Indian rugs and shabby, comfortable furniture. Both Shep and the playful antelope followed.

"Come with me," Uncle John said, "and I will introduce you to the boss of the Circle K."

This puzzled Bob. He thought that his uncle was the boss. But he said nothing and followed into an oblong room almost filled with a long table and narrow benches.

18

"This is where we eat," his uncle said. Then he led the way on into a warm and cheerful kitchen. Good smells hung about it so heavily that Bob's mouth watered.

"This is Cookie," Uncle John said. "You'd better be good to him, because he rules the roost around here. If you make him mad he won't feed you, and then you'd starve to death."

Cookie grinned. He looked to Bob as though he wouldn't get angry very easily. His cheeks were pink and he had a round, fat stomach. In fact, he looked as though he liked his own cooking very much.

"Bob wants to be a real cowboy," Uncle John told Cookie, a twinkle in his eyes.

Cookie put his hands on his hips and stared down at Bob. "That means," he said slowly, "that I'll have a roustabout for a few months. Young man, if you work hard, you and I will get along all right. I like your looks. But mind, I don't stand for any monkey business. When I need wood, I have to have wood, right pronto!"

Bob looked at his uncle questioningly.

"He means," said his uncle in his usual brisk tone, "that you are to be the boy who does odd chores around the ranch. One of your special jobs will be to carry wood for the cooking. All cowboys start by being roustabouts."

Bob gulped. This did not fit at all into his idea of being a cowboy.

19

"But when do I start being a cowboy?" he asked. "When do I get to ride horses and punch cattle?"

His uncle's lips twitched at the corners. "Oh, that comes later," he said. "Much later. Probably not at all this summer. Riding is dangerous business. I wouldn't want you to get hurt."

"I won't get hurt!" Bob cried. "I'll be careful and I'll help with the cattle and make myself very useful."

"You can start making yourself useful right now then," said Cookie. "Take that iron bar on the bench outside and whack it against the iron triangle hanging near the door. That will bring the men in to chuck."

Bob went outside and jangled the bar against the triangle. From the barn and corrals and beyond, he saw several men start to hurry toward the log house. Bob's heart leaped at the sight of these real cowboys. Each of them wore high-heeled boots and a wide hat pushed to the back of his head. All wore neckerchiefs, and a few wore chaps. Some were tall, some were short, but all were lean and sturdy looking.

They came to the long bench against the porch and washed their hands and faces in the row of washbasins that stood there. Then they slicked their hair and headed for the dining room.

"Fellows, let me introduce you to the new 'ranny' of the Circle K," Montana drawled. "Bob, this long hombre

20

built like a snake on stilts is Crowbait. This guy with a face like a hoss is called Happy because he's always sad. And this would-be cowpuncher that sort of drags the ground when he walks is Shorty. He's had a hoss under him so long his legs are warped."

Bob bowed politely, uncertain how to respond to this manner of introduction. Each of the men grinned and said howdy.

The cowboys went to the long table and threw their legs over the benches. Immediately dishes of food began to move down the table. Each man piled his plate high, passed the dish along, and started eating. It was plain to see that this part of the day's work was a serious business to these men.

Bob sat next to his uncle at the head of the table and almost forgot to eat, he was so busy watching. Never had he seen such interesting men. Shorty, he decided, must be the clown of the ranch for he had a jolly twinkle in his eyes and chuckled whenever he spoke. Crowbait, he didn't like so well, because there was a mean tone to the way he called Montana, "our movie cowboy," when he asked him to pass the spuds. Of course, Bob thought, Montana did look like a moving-picture hero, all right. He guessed Crowbait must be jealous. He decided that Happy must be the strong, silent type. Scarcely a word came from him, and his long face wore such a melancholy expression that Bob wondered if some secret sorrow weighed on his heart.

As they were eating their apple pie, Uncle John said, "The boys are going to break horses tomorrow. You may watch, Bob, if you wish—after your chores are done."

"Chores?" Bob questioned.

"Of course. Carrying in wood and water. Whatever Cookie wants you to do."

"Oh!" came faintly from Bob's throat, but the more exciting part of his uncle's statement swept the slight disappointment over chores from his mind.

"Gee whillikers!" he cried. "Then I start right in learning how to break horses!"

"Yes," said his uncle, "you can start learning how, but don't start putting what you learn into practice. Breaking horses is dangerous business. I want to send you back to your father and mother in one piece."

"You mean that sometimes horses break people?" Bob asked.

"And how!" Shorty spoke up. "I tried to break an outlaw hoss once. But instead, he broke me. My leg, in three places. I've been out of rodeos ever since. And me the best rider in forty-nine states."

At this modest remark a shout went up from the other cowboys.

"Cowboys like to brag about themselves," Bob's uncle

explained. "But none of them is as good as he claims to be."

"I'm the only one as can make such a boast truthfully," said Crowbait.

"Ho!" Montana cried. "Crowbait's apt to get calluses from patting himself on the back. He's been bucked off so often he's loosened till he plumb rattles when he walks."

"Is that so?" Crowbait retorted. "Well, the last time I saw you ride, soon as your hoss bogged its head, you grabbed the saddle horn and nearly pulled it out by the roots, trying to hang on. That animal was sure full of bedsprings, all right. I can see it yet—the way it hid its head and kicked the lid off. And when it warped its backbone you went flying off, your legs kicking like a flying frog with the jerks."

Cowboy talk, Bob decided, must be almost like a foreign language.

"Get your chores done pronto," Montana told him, "and we'll take a little look-see about the place."

Cookie told him what to do—fill the woodbox and the water buckets and carry the table scraps to the chickens.

After supper and chores, Bob went with Montana on a short tour of inspection about the ranch buildings. He saw the huge storeroom where supplies were kept. It was like a small, well-stocked store. He stopped to look at the row of saddles thrown across a fence rail. He saw the bunkhouse where the men slept, with its round-bellied stove in the center of the room and the rows of two-tiered bunks built against the walls.

He stared fascinated at the array of branding irons hanging on the blacksmith-shop wall. Montana showed him where the Circle K brand had been burned into the door—a K inside a circle.

"Why!" cried Bob. "That makes an 'O.K.' Why don't you call this the O.K. Ranch? That's what it is, all right."

Montana stroked his chin and grinned. "I reckon you're right. This spread is O.K. But brands were used before that term was."

"I'm going to call it the O.K. Ranch just the same," Bob said. "When I write Mother and Dad tonight, I'll draw the brand mark at the top of the page."

BRAND
CIRCLE-K

2. A Horse with Bedsprings

THE NEXT MORNING Bob was up earlier than he had been ever in his life before. But even though it was not yet five o'clock, the men were eating breakfast. Led by the savory smells of coffee, bacon, and pancakes, Bob hurried to the dining room. There he found the cowboys, shoving food into their mouths as if they had to catch a train.

"Howdy, there," Montana called out. "I didn't think you'd be such a sleepyhead. You'll never make a top hand if you lie abed mornings."

Bob thought he was anything but a sleepyhead to be up before five o'clock. Evidently it was a cowboy custom to get up with the birds.

"I was going to let you sleep this morning," his uncle said as Bob slipped into his place. "I thought you were most likely tired."

"Oh, I don't want to sleep," Bob cried. "I want to see what's going on. And today I was going to start to learn to break horses."

At this everyone laughed, but Bob could not see that there was anything funny about what he had said. Cookie piled his plate with hot cakes and bacon and put a cup of coffee before him.

"Oh, I don't drink coffee, thank you," Bob told him. "I'd rather have milk, please."

Again everyone laughed. This time Bob was sure he had not said anything funny.

"We don't have milk here, except what we get out of cans," his uncle stated.

"Don't have milk!" exclaimed Bob. "But you have millions of cows. I should think you would have millions of gallons of milk."

"We raise cattle for beef," his uncle explained. "We don't bother with milk cows. Of course some of the cows have milk for their calves, but those cows are quite wild. We couldn't milk them without roping and tying them, and that would be a lot of trouble."

"Oh!" said Bob. "I guess I'll just take water with my meals then." But it still seemed strange to him that on a cattle ranch there should be no milk except canned milk.

After breakfast the men sauntered out to the big corral. Bob hurried to bring in wood and water and to carry scraps to the chickens. He didn't linger around the kitchen for fear Cookie would find more chores for him to do. He hastened after Montana, taking long steps like his and trying to make his legs wishbone shaped, the way most of the cowboys' legs were.

Already Bob had picked Montana for his favorite cowpuncher. He liked the way Montana looked and acted, the jaunty air with which the cowboy wore his wide hat on the back of his head and the way his jeans hung low on his slim hips. He admired Montana's fancy high-heeled boots with their white-leather trimming and stitching and the way this top hand did everything with an easy grace, never seeming to be in a hurry, yet making every motion count.

The young, unbroken horses had been driven in from the range and were now gathered in the larger corral, where they crowded together for comfort and protection. Montana climbed to the top of the high gate separating the two corrals and looked over the frightened animals.

"Have yourself an 'opery seat' up here with Shorty," he suggested to Bob. "If you hanker to be a broncobuster, you'd better start learning right now."

Bob clambered up the poles and perched beside Shorty, who instantly won his liking by saying, "If you want to be a broncobuster, Montana's about the best teacher you could find. He has more hoss sense than a dozen ordinary cowmen."

"I knew right away that Montana was good," Bob echoed, pleased to have his judgment confirmed.

"He's sizing the hosses up now," Shorty went on. "He can tell just by looking at one whether it will be a good cow pony, a good roundup animal, just an ordinary work hoss, or only fit for rodeo."

"Do different horses do different things?" Bob asked. "I thought that after a horse was broken it could do most anything."

"Oh, no! Hosses differ considerable in their talents," Shorty explained. "A good cow pony—that is, one that can be used for roping cattle—is considered tops. Hosses that can be trained to do that sort of work are rare. They're really prized on the range."

"How can a broncobuster tell which horses are going to be good?" Bob asked.

Shorty shrugged. "Just hoss sense," he said. "See that bay over there?" He pointed at an animal crowding against the others. Its nostrils were distended, its eyes wide and bloodshot with terror. "That's a good hoss. Plenty of spirit and speed. Intelligence, too. The things that's needed to make a good cow pony."

Even to Bob, who knew nothing about horses, the handsome animal looked good.

"If you want a horse with spirit, there's one over there." Bob pointed to an animal that was on its hind legs, screaming and pawing at the poles of the corral.

"That hoss is plumb full of meanness," Shorty said. "An outlaw—loco. There's some hosses that never can be gentled. He's one. He'll be saved for rodeo work, if he doesn't turn out to be a killer."

Bob looked startled. "Horses don't ever kill people, do they?" he cried. "I mean, on purpose?"

Shorty nodded. "Every once in a while we find a killer. But they're rare. See that big chestnut high-stepping it over at the other side of the corral?"

Bob nodded.

"Well," Shorty chuckled, "there's one place where Montana's sense failed him. He's made his brags that he can break that hoss. Me, I have a mite of hoss sense, too. I used to be a broncobuster before a bronc busted me. I know that hoss can't be gentled."

"What are they doing now?" Bob asked. Montana had climbed down from the gate, and several of the cowboys had entered the corral where the horses were.

"They're going to cut out that little bay for Montana to gentle first," Shorty answered. "I guessed she would be the one. Montana's probably picked her to train for his own cow pony."

After about five minutes of wild confusion among that

29

herd of horses, the high gate between the corrals swung open and the bay, with ears perked up and head and tail held high, was forced to enter the circular corral alone. As the gate closed, she stood motionless except for the quivering of glossy muscles and the motion of the widened nostrils and eyes.

Montana approached the horse, talking to her in soothing tones while his rope circled over her head. Suddenly the rope whined and settled around the bay's neck. The horse jerked back with tensed haunches, and Montana's high-heeled boots plowed the hard dirt as he pulled with all his might. He pulled until he could get his rope wound tightly around the snubbing post in the middle of the corral.

Bob noticed that the post had a groove midway of its height and asked Shorty about it.

"Worn that way," Shorty told him. "Worn by ropes."

The terrified horse shrieked wildly until her breath was cut off by the cruel rope. Then she threw herself about in a useless effort to fight this thing that was choking the life from her. But the struggle went on for only a short time. When the horse stood motionless, Montana approached and loosened the rope around the animal's neck. She stood panting for a few moments, then again started to pull back. Once more the rope tightened. When the bay stopped straining, Montana loosed the noose. Shorty nodded with satisfaction. "The bay is going to catch on quick," he said. "Already she's learned the lesson of the rope. She won't fight it again."

"The lesson of the rope?" Bob asked. "What's that?"

"It's the first thing a hoss has to learn," Shorty explained. "The first step in training a hoss is to lasso it. Naturally the animal pulls back on the loop around its neck, and the harder it pulls the tighter the loop is drawn. It isn't a pleasant experience, and a hoss almost never fights the rope again. Just the feel of a rope on its neck is generally enough to make a hoss stand still."

Montana was standing near the bay's head, stroking her glossy neck, rubbing her ears. All the while he talked to her soothingly.

"He's letting her get used to the man smell," Shorty explained. "All animals that have run wild are scared to death of the man smell, but they get used to it in time."

A little later Montana took a saddle blanket and tossed it lightly on the bay's back, then drew it off. He repeated this time and again, talking all the while. The animal quivered each time the blanket touched her flesh, but she did not attempt to fight, for the rope was still on her neck.

"What will he do now?" Bob asked eagerly.

"Put the saddle on her back and take it off," Shorty replied. "He'll do that until the bay gets used to its feel."

At a signal from Montana, Crowbait and Happy approached the horse. Crowbait slipped the noose from the pony's neck. Happy gripped the bay's ears and twisted them and held her head tightly against his chest while Crowbait helped Montana cinch up the saddle.

"Happy twists the pony's ears to take her attention from what's happening to her back," Shorty explained.

Montana stepped to the side of the horse, close to her head. He twisted the left-hand stirrup toward him. The reins were in his left hand. Suddenly his weight was in the stirrup and his right leg was flung over the saddle. At the same time the two cowboys leaped aside. For a moment the bay stood motionless, then her head went between her forelegs and she seemed to explode all over the place.

Bob gripped the pole and his heart almost stopped beating. He thought surely Montana would be killed. Even if he were not thrown from that crazily leaping animal, it seemed certain that his spine would be cracked.

But somehow the cowboy managed to stay on. And it seemed not to be difficult to him. He held the reins with only one hand while with the other he held his hat. Then, when the bay finally showed signs of weakening, Montana flapped his hat and yelled and scratched the bay's sides with his spurs. She leaped about a bit more, but

*The bay exploded
all over the place*

soon her head came up again and it was plain to see that, for the time being, the fight was all gone from her.

Montana dismounted and patted the pony's neck.

"A good ride," everyone told him.

"Is the bay broken now?" Bob asked.

"Oh, no," Shorty chuckled. "She'll put on a show like this every day for a week or ten days, most likely. Then she'll decide that man is master after all. Most hosses have to find that out someday, but a lot of them are slow about giving in."

3. Cowboy or Tenderfoot?

BOB set his alarm for four-thirty. The first few mornings it was next to impossible to drag himself from his comfortable bed, but he forced himself to do it. If getting up at this hour was part of a cowboy's life, he was determined to go through with it, even if, so far, he was allowed to do only the disagreeable things and none of the thrilling ones. He had no liking for roustabout chores, but he did them grimly, with only an occasional reminder from Cookie. He lived for the day when he would be allowed to ride a horse and go with the cowboys on their exciting duties.

Bob was all agog with curiosity as to what those duties might be. He hated to make a nuisance of himself by asking questions all the time, especially since Crowbait told him, "A good cowboy uses his eyes a lot and his mouth mighty little," and that "airin' one's lungs" was frowned upon. So, by watching and listening, he learned that when the men went to gather the "cavy," they brought in the horses; that a line-rider's job was to "ride the range" and see that none of his employer's cattle strayed off the ranch or others strayed in; that "cutting out the weaners" meant driving calves five or six months old into a pasture apart from their mothers.

It was Shorty who explained the use of each article of cowboy wearing apparel. Bob had thought that most of the things cowmen wore served a somewhat decorative purpose, but he learned differently.

"Take the neckerchief, for instance." Shorty fingered his red bandanna. "It isn't worn for looks. It has a heap of uses besides keeping my neck from getting sunburned. I can tie it up over my nose to keep the dust from choking me or I can dip it in water to wash and cool my face on a hot day."

Shorty took off his large Stetson hat and fingered it lovingly.

"A cowboy's ten-gallon hat is one of the very most precious things he owns," he went on. "I paid thirty dollars for mine. And it has a dozen uses besides keeping my brains from getting curdled by the sun. I use it to haze hosses, or corral spooky livestock. And when I'm riding a bucking hoss it comes in useful to help balance myself. It's a handy drinking cup sometimes, too."

"I suppose then," Bob broke in, "that the chaps you men wear aren't just for show-off, either."

"Nothing a regular cowman wears is for show-off," Shorty answered indignantly. "Chaps protect a rider from weather and brush. And they help keep his legs from getting hurt if he's thrown or pushed against a barbed-wire fence."

"The thing I like best about a cowboy's outfit," Bob sighed, "is his boots. My, I wish I had a pair of cowboy boots. I thought maybe Dad would send me some, but he doesn't seem to think I need them."

Shorty thrust his feet out and stared at his elaborately stitched, high-heeled boots.

"A 'waddy's' boots are even more precious than his hat," Shorty said. "They're the most expensive part of his riggin'. No self-respecting ranny would wear store boots; they have to be made to order. The high heels keep the feet from slipping through the stirrups and help him dig in when he's roping from the ground. The toes are pointed like this to make it easier to pick up a stirrup."

"Why do all the boots have such fancy stitching and trimming?" Bob asked.

"That's to make the tops stiff enough so they won't wrinkle at the ankle," Shorty explained.

"I hadn't any idea," Bob exclaimed, "that everything about a cowboy's rigging was so useful!"

*Bob even practiced
roping the chickens*

"The most useful thing of all," Shorty told him, "is the rope. Any waddy is lost without his lariat. He does most everything but eat with it."

"That's what Montana said," Bob cried eagerly. "He's teaching me how to rope. I practice every day."

"I noticed," Shorty said approvingly. "You've got a real knack for it. I don't believe I ever saw anyone catch on so quick."

Bob was so pleased with Shorty's praise that he practiced more industriously than ever. Montana gave him an old lariat for his own. With this he roped fence posts, stumps, chickens. He even used Shep and the pet antelope whenever they would stand still, but they soon became bored with the game and avoided Bob when he had his rope with him.

Bob's first week on the ranch sped by in almost no time, it seemed to him. Each day was much like the one before, yet there was usually something exciting happening. After he did his roustabout chores, including the potato peeling which he heartily disliked, he would hurry out and watch the men breaking horses. This seemed to go on nearly all of the time. Some of the ponies were being trained now to be ridden while the rider twirled a rope. Later they would be taught to pull back enough to hold the rope taut after the rider caught a calf in his loop.

Horsebreaking was very exciting for a while, but after the first week Bob did not care to sit all day on the top rail of the corral and watch the bucking. He wished, as he sat on a stump listlessly twirling his rope, that he could be doing something on the ranch besides chores. Why was his uncle so afraid he might get hurt? He could take care of himself. And how grand it would be to write home about something he—not others—had done.

Shep was good company but had his work to do. Even the dog, Bob lamented, was important on the ranch. No wonder Shep preferred the excitement of working with the cowboys on the range to playing around the house with Bob.

"Why such a long face, partner?" Montana asked as he swung along. "Getting tired of cowboy life?"

"I can't get tired of it before I've started," Bob answered bitterly. "My uncle won't let me do anything but chores. I don't think he even likes me."

"Ho!" Montana snorted. "Stop feeling sorry for yourself. Of course the boss likes you. He's just taking the responsibility for your safety too seriously. And I reckon maybe he's forgotten how it feels to be a kid."

Bob looked up and smiled, grateful for the understanding he sensed in Montana's tone.

"Just keep plugging along with your rope," the cowboy advised. "Do your chores without being told, keep

40

your eyes and ears open to learn all you can, and one of these days the chance will come along to prove the stuff you're made of."

Just then Cookie came out to the well. As he was going back to the kitchen with his bucket full of water, the antelope came leaping around the house and playfully butted him, splashing the water all over his legs. Bob and Montana could not keep from laughing.

"You imp!" Cookie cried, shaking his fist at the playful animal. "That's what you ought to be called—Imp!"

"Oh, no!" Bob shouted. "I've already named him. We'll call him Button, because he's always buttin' people around."

"Well," agreed Cookie, filling his pail again, "that isn't bad."

The pleasantest time of day to Bob was after supper. Then the men squatted on their haunches or sat with their backs against the bunkhouse and told stories or sang cowboy songs to the accompaniment of Happy's guitar. The songs were usually mournful, like Happy's favorite:

> Oh, bury me not on the lone prairie,
> Where the wild coyotes will howl o'er me,
> Where the rattlesnakes hiss and the winds blow free,
> Oh, bury me not on the lone prairie!

These songs filled Bob's heart with a vast longing for

41

something, though he did not know just what. The cowboys' stories, too, he thoroughly enjoyed. One, especially, excited his fancy. It was Shorty, the most talkative of the men, who told it.

"I have the story straight from a friend of a couple of trappers who found gold back in the hills near their cabin," Shorty said. "One of the trappers was later killed by Injuns. The other one was wounded. The wounded one managed to crawl to Fort Laramie. Before he died, he gave a description of the gold mine and showed some of the nuggets he took from it."

"I've heard tell," Crowbait drawled, "that Lost Cabin Mine is supposed to be on this very ranch. And it's chuck-full of gold."

Bob was so excited by this story that his hair prickled on his scalp. He resolved then and there someday to search for the mine. But when, later on, he confided his plan to Montana, the top hand advised, "Don't pay any attention to Shorty's tall tales. He was just airin' his lungs. If there was any truth in the story, which I doubt, how would anyone know which of the dozens of gullies or canyons back in the hills might be it?"

"But that one over there—that sort of V-shaped one—is called Lost Cabin Canyon!" Bob exclaimed. "That must be the one."

"Don't prove anything to me," Montana grinned,

"'cept whoever named it had a good imagination. Most every ranch I've been on has a Lost Cabin Creek, or Lost Cabin Mountain, or Lost Cabin something else on it. Seems like the old-timers were mighty careless about their cabins."

Bob was disappointed that Montana put no stock in Shorty's story.

"Don't fret about it," the foreman told Bob. "There'll be plenty of exciting things to do later. The calf roundup and the branding. Plenty of things."

"Uh-huh." Bob nodded absently.

Lost Cabin Canyon was pulling him like a magnet. He knew that he would not be satisfied until he explored it.

4. A Would-Be Cowboy

Bob hit the floor with a bang at daybreak on Monday, even before his alarm clock stopped ringing. He had a pleasant feeling that something exciting was going to happen to him today.

Then at breakfast it happened. Quite casually his uncle turned to Montana and said, "I think Bob has earned the privilege of riding a horse. Will you saddle one for him when you finish eating?"

Bob was so happy he wanted to turn somersaults. He was so excited he could scarcely eat. His enthusiasm was dampened a little when his uncle added, "Mind you pick a gentle horse, Montana. Perhaps one of the older work animals."

"But I don't want an old slowpoke!" Bob could not hold the words back.

John Benton turned from Montana to his nephew.

"I'm responsible for your safety, Bob," he said in his usual firm tone. "You're not used to horses, so I must be sure the animal you ride is safe."

Bob swallowed his disappointment. After all, he reminded himself, he was lucky to have any horse. Perhaps later he would be given a pony that would go galloping over the ranch with him.

Montana winked at him understandingly. Then he said, as he left the table, "Don't worry, boss. I'll pick a good hoss and I'll ride him myself till all the spook's out of him."

"What does he mean by 'the spook is out of him'?" Bob asked his uncle.

"Most horses that haven't been ridden for some time act rather skittish the first time someone mounts them," Uncle John explained. "The cowboys call that skittishness 'spook.' Even the work horses that are used every day during the busy season have a lot of spook in them in the morning."

"I'd like a spooky horse," Bob cried. "It sounds exciting."

"It might be more exciting than you think," his uncle remarked dryly.

"But if I'm going to be a cowboy I'll have to know how to ride lively horses," Bob protested.

His uncle looked at him through narrowed eyes. "It

45

takes time to become a cowboy," he said slowly. "But it takes more than that. A person must have certain qualities to be a good cowboy."

John Benton paused a moment, then went on thoughtfully, "A good cowboy must be a real man. He must have courage and dependability. He mustn't be afraid of hardships and he must know what to do in an emergency." He looked straight at Bob. "You'll have to prove that you have those qualities before I let you endanger your life and my property. See what I mean?"

Bob nodded. He wanted to cry, "I'll prove that I have them, if you'll only give me a chance!" But the words stuck in his throat.

Uncle John patted him on the head. "After all, you're only a boy," he said kindly. "I wouldn't expect anyone to be a cowboy until he's a full-grown man."

Bob gritted his teeth. He wished that his uncle would stop treating him like a little fellow who should be eating in a high chair.

He heard Montana, who had gone to the barnyard, give a shrill whistle and he raced out. Shep, sensing Bob's excitement, ran around barking; Button leaped about, butting the men.

"This is Calico," Montana grinned, rubbing the pony's neck and velvety nose.

Bob jumped up and down.

46

"Calico is a keen name," he said, as he looked at the brown patches on the white horse. "Is he a lively horse?" He looked at Montana hopefully.

"Lively enough," Montana answered. "He's well-trained. I broke him myself."

Uncle John had followed Bob to the barnyard. "You may ride around the yard for an hour," he said.

Bob's eyes widened with disappointment. "But I wanted to ride around the ranch," he wailed.

"I'm sorry," his uncle said rather coolly, "but none of the men has time to go with you. If you don't care to ride around the barnyard, I'll have Montana turn Calico out again."

"Oh, no!" Bob cried. "I'll like riding around the yard. Really I will."

Mr. Benton turned to Montana. "When you have time, I want you to show Bob how to take off the saddle and care for the horse. Later on you can show him how to saddle his own pony."

Bob grinned his gratitude. That was what he wanted. To be shown how to do the things a cowboy did for himself.

"Climb aboard," Montana told him.

Eagerly Bob ran to the left side of the horse, put his right foot in the stirrup and threw his other foot over the saddle as he thought he remembered having seen

47

horsemen do in the movies. He looked up as a great roar came from the throats of Montana and Uncle John and from Shorty, Crowbait, and Happy, who had just come from the barn.

Bob was sitting in the saddle all right, but he was facing Calico's tail! His face turned red and his eyes smarted.

"I shouldn't be surprised if the scenery is prettier going backward," Crowbait remarked.

Montana reached up to help Bob from the saddle.

"Don't let it bother you," he said, trying to straighten out his face. "I've seen grown men do the same thing."

He swung Bob down.

"First take hold of the steering gear—the reins—with your left hand, take hold of the stirrup with your right hand and pull it toward the shoulder of the horse."

Silently Bob did as he was told, glad to have his crimson face turned away from his audience.

"Now put your *left* foot in the stirrup," the cowboy went on. "Take hold of the saddle horn, throw your right leg up, and at the same time pull yourself up by the saddle horn. There, see how simple it is? And you're headed in the right direction. Keep hold of the reins and make a clicking sound like this with your tongue and press lightly with your knees."

It made Bob feel very foolish and self-conscious to

48

have all the men standing there, watching him. Even Cookie had come out and stood, egg beater in one hand and a big grin on his face.

"Ride 'em, cowboy!" he cried.

Calico started out, but not very enthusiastically. He walked as sedately as if he expected to step on eggs any minute.

"Would you like a little glue on the seat of your pants?" Crowbait asked.

"Stay aboard and don't let his bucking scare you." Shorty added his bit to the clever remarks.

Bob took their teasing with a grin. He knew that every cowboy had to take his share of kidding and that no one admired the one who got grouchy.

He yanked on the reins in a businesslike manner to show that he was really riding, instead of just sitting on top of a horse. Calico jerked his head angrily.

Montana walked up beside the horse and said in a low tone, "Don't yank on the reins that way, Bob. It makes a hoss mad. Just let the rein touch his neck on the side you want to turn. That's what's called neck-reining. That's the way to steer a Circle K pony."

Bob tried this method and found that it worked.

"I reckon he'll do," he heard Shorty say. "He knows how to neck-rein a horse. He don't yank on the bit the way most tenderfeet do."

Bob and Montana exchanged a meaningful glance.

After a while the audience grew tired of watching Bob ride around and around the barnyard and drifted away to their own work.

"I'll be back later to show you how to take the saddle off," Montana told Bob. "Any cowboy that's worth the name takes good care of his hoss. Better care than he takes of himself."

Bob was left alone to ride. Calico, plainly bored with this exercise, walked more and more slowly. Bob kicked his heels against the pony's ribs and cried "giddap," but Calico only flipped his ears and almost stopped.

Then Shep came into the barnyard. He perked up his ears at the sight of a cow pony traveling at a snail's pace. Not being used to seeing this sort of thing, he decided that it was his duty to do something about the matter. So he started to bark and nip the horse's heels. At that, Calico kicked out and started to run.

Bob had thought that this was what he wanted, but now he changed his mind. The horse jogged up and down until Bob thought his head would snap off his neck. He tried holding the reins loosely, as Montana had told him to do, but Calico only jogged harder. Then he seized the pommel of the saddle with one hand and tightened the reins with the other. At once Calico changed his gait and began to go in a smooth, easy motion that made Bob feel as if he were riding in a rocking chair. It frightened him a little at first, and he did not know whether or not he could stick to the saddle. Then he found that if he held himself rather loosely, instead of as stiff as a ramrod, this galloping motion was really enjoyable. Or would be if only he could be sailing over the soft green grasslands of the ranch instead of around and around the small enclosure.

Finally Calico slowed down, and Shep grew tired of pestering him and ran away. Bob looked at the gate. The fastening was at the top. He could reach it without dismounting. He guided the pony over and reached down, just to see if he could work it. The gate started to swing outward toward the grasslands and freedom, where the breezes seemed to be fresher and adventure beckoned. Bob swung the gate back into place and went riding slowly around the barnyard once more.

The next time around he tried the gate again. It still swung out easily and temptingly. Once more Bob pulled it back into place. The third time around he let the gate swing out. Clear open it swung, but this time Bob did not pull it shut. Instead, he let his rein gently touch the right side of Calico's neck, and the pony stepped through, out into the free world.

For a moment Bob's heart almost stopped beating with the excitement of what he was doing. He tried to still his conscience by telling himself that he was not actually disobeying his uncle. No one had told him not to open the gate. Besides, he could ride now. Hadn't he gone galloping? He could stay on a horse whether it trotted or galloped. And now that he knew how to manage a horse, why shouldn't he ride where the riding was some fun? If he proved to his uncle that he was able to take care of himself, perhaps he would be treated more like a man. And he would have something to write home about. He could tell them he had been out galloping over the range.

Calico, too, seemed glad to be free of the uninteresting confines of the barnyard. He snorted, jerked his head, perked up his ears, and started to trot. This was not to Bob's liking. He did not care to have his head snapped this way. He wished that Shep would nip Calico's heels again to start him to galloping. But the dog had remained behind.

Finally Bob found that by pulling on both reins and kicking the pony's ribs he could get into the gallop again. Once more his body adjusted itself to the motion. It was delightful! He threw his head back to enjoy the feel of the rush of air against his face. Galloping across the grassy plains, with the wind raising his hair and the tang of sage in his nostrils, was even more fun than he had imagined.

He reined Calico toward the chalk buttes that loomed like ancient fortresses against the blue mountains. On a galloping horse he could make the trip in a short while, explore those interesting sandstone piles, and be back at the ranch in time for lunch.

He would tell his uncle quite openly about his adventure. Uncle John had said that a cowboy must prove himself. Well, wasn't that exactly what he was doing? After proving that he could ride and take care of himself, it stood to reason that his uncle would then allow him to ride any time and wherever he wished.

Bob's thoughts were very pleasant indeed. His chest swelled as he gazed out at a wild, free world and felt himself to be king of all he could see.

The chalk buttes crawled nearer. Calico slackened his pace. Bob realized that a horse could not go on galloping forever, no matter how pleasant the motion was to the rider. Probably the animal was thirsty. When they came to a stream he would allow the horse to drink, and while exploring the buttes he would let Calico graze on the green grass.

He rode by a pasture where a herd of horses grazed. Old Molly, the bell mare, looked at Bob with startled, accusing eyes as though she knew that he was doing something wrong.

Then a jack rabbit leaped in front of Calico. The horse

snorted in terror and reared to his hind legs. Bob, taken entirely by surprise, slid back. He kept right on sliding until he slid over the pony's tail and hit the ground with a bump.

For a moment he was too dazed to move. Then he got up slowly, rubbed himself where he had landed, and looked after Calico, running for all he was worth. Bob hoped that Calico would turn and come back when he

*The horse reared
and Bob slid back*

got over his fright. But the horse was soon out of sight and Bob was left standing alone, out in the middle of the Circle K Ranch.

What should he do? Should he start walking back to the ranch house, or should he go on to the buttes which were so close now? He decided that he would explore the buttes before walking back home. Perhaps another chance would not come very soon, now that he had not done such a good job of proving his ability to take care of himself!

5. Adventure on the Range

Bob's HEART lifted as he walked toward the buttes. The song of the meadow larks was the sweetest sound he had ever heard. He looked at the herds of cattle grazing peacefully on the hillsides and at the colts that kicked up their heels, nipped each other playfully, and raced the length of the pasture. The wind rippled the silky grass and brought the fragrance of wild flowers and sage to his nostrils.

The great sandstone buttes loomed like ancient castles and fortresses. Climbing about among them, the place became in reality an ancient battlement to Bob. He found natural rooms, caves, and fortifications. In his interest he almost forgot his uneasiness over being left afoot so far from the ranch house.

He saw a bit of flint sticking up in the sandy dirt. When he had pried it loose, he found that he was holding a perfect arrowhead. Bob's heart leaped with excitement. Indians had actually been in this very place then! He looked about almost uneasily, as if a feathered headdress might pop up from behind one of the rocks. Then he told himself not to be silly. No Indians were lurking around a cattle ranch. They had long ago been driven from this region and were now safe and civilized on their own reservations.

There were only two things to mar Bob's enjoyment— the thought of the punishment that would likely come to him for leaving the barnyard without permission, and the increasing emptiness of his stomach. If only he had brought along a lunch and something to drink!

The sun was riding high overhead, and Bob decided that he had better be starting back to the ranch house. Maybe if he ran part of the way he could make it in time for lunch. He started on a dogtrot but soon slowed down, as the running caused a pain in his side and increased his thirst.

He walked endlessly without seeming to get anywhere. The sun beat down on his bare head and he had never been so hot and uncomfortable. All that he could think of was how thirsty he was. He remembered the cool stream that ran past the ranch house. Surely he should be coming to it soon. But the willows and aspens which lined its banks were nowhere in sight. He had not dreamed that there was such an expanse of emptiness on the ranch. So much space without trees or buildings. But there was nothing to do but keep putting one foot in front of the other, no matter how tired or thirsty he was.

It seemed to Bob that he had been walking for hours. He thought it strange that he had not come in sight of the ranch house. He decided to climb a mound-shaped hill he saw and have a look around to get his bearings. But when he came to the top of the hill and gazed in every direction he saw no buildings. No heartening wisp of smoke to guide him. No flash of the silver blades of the windmill. No familiar landmark. Nothing but gently sloping hills.

Then he knew that he was lost. He looked back to see the buttes in order to get his bearings. But they were nowhere in sight. It was as if the ground had opened and swallowed them.

Terror, such as Bob had never known, gripped him. Lost! It was the most helpless, frightening feeling in the world. The strange, unfamiliar land suddenly became terrifying and unfriendly. He stared about wildly. Panic paralyzed his mind and legs.

Finally a bit of common sense came to his rescue. It was broad daylight. There really was nothing to fear, he told himself. No wild animals or Indians or anything that could harm him. He must try to figure things out. Get his bearings. Then he would commence walking again and after a while he could come to the ranch house. That was all there was to it—except the reckoning for his adventure. He would welcome that now, if only it would bring him to the ranch house and to human beings.

A clump of bushes in the distance looked as though they might be willows. That would mean water! And if he found a stream he could follow it until it brought him to people.

Bob's feet were blistered now, and his thirst was almost unbearable, but on and on he trudged toward the bushes.

When he finally came to the willows, sure enough, there was a small stream. He threw himself on his stomach, put his mouth to the water, and drank and drank and drank. Then he dashed the cool water over his hot face. He took off his shoes and splashed his feet in the pleasant water until the fire was gone from them. While he was doing this, he pulled some wild, coarse grasses growing beside the stream and nibbled the tender ends.

It was pleasant here in the cool shade with the happy gurgle of the brook. Bob felt some of his fear evaporating as he sat beside the friendly stream. He would rest awhile. He lay back on the soft grass with his hands under his head and stared up at the powder-puff clouds as they floated lazily by, forming interesting shapes.

Suddenly he heard a fierce, angry snort. He jumped. A fiercer snort brought him to his feet. Looking about, he saw a terrible animal snorting and pawing the ground on the other side of the stream.

Bob screamed. It was a mad bull, and he had heard how dangerous they were. The bulls he had seen before always had been on the opposite side of a strong fence. And he had never seen one so gigantic or ferocious looking. This one seemed to fill the whole world. Terror froze him to the spot as he stared at the snorting beast, pawing the ground and glowering with mean, bloodshot eyes. Then the bull started lunging across the stream.

Suddenly Bob's feet found wings. He caught sight of a pile of boulders a short distance away and fairly flew to this small fortress. Just in time he leaped behind the largest rock.

Then followed the most terrifying and wearing game. Bob dodged around the rock while the bull snorted and pawed and tried to reach this creature who had dared to invade his domain.

Would the animal never tire? Would this grim game of hide-and-seek go on, Bob wondered, until he dropped in his tracks for the bull to gore?

Just when it seemed that he could not stand the weariness and terror another minute, there reached Bob's ears

*Just in time Bob leaped
behind the rock*

the most welcome sound he had ever heard. The thud of galloping hoofs. Over his shoulder he saw a rider rising and falling as he crossed the uneven ground and growing larger as he came closer.

Now he could see the horseman more clearly. It was Montana!

As the thud of hoofs reached the bull's ears, he turned, giving Bob time to regain his breath, then went pounding to meet this new invader.

Bob watched, expecting to see Montana draw his six-shooter to lay the bull low. His heart leaped to his throat when he saw that, instead, the cowboy started to whirl his rope over his head.

Was Montana crazy, Bob thought, using a frail rope against that gigantic animal? If his first throw should miss, his horse might be gored, for they were out in the open with nothing to hide behind.

But Montana did not miss. His rope snaked out close to the ground, caught the forepaws of the heavy beast and sent him somersaulting. Then, as the bull tried to rise with his forelegs doubled under him, Montana circled him until the rope was wound around and around his legs and the creature lay bellowing in helpless anger.

As Montana galloped nearer, Bob ran to meet him. The cowboy reached down, seized Bob under the armpits, and swung him up behind the saddle.

63

"Hang onto my waist," Montana shouted, as he urged his pony to gallop faster.

The wind whistled past Bob's face, lifting his hair as he grasped Montana in a bear grip.

After they had galloped for some distance, Montana drew the badly winded pony to its haunches before a high gate. He reached down and lifted the wire which held it, spurred the pony through, and swiftly swung the gate to again.

Then he paused and turned to look back into the pasture they had left. Bob looked, too, and saw the bull slowly rising from the ground. The beast shook himself, bellowed twice, then lumbered away in the opposite direction.

"Reckon the play's plumb took out of him," Montana said. "But I wasn't going to chance waiting to see. I knew he'd break that rope in short order."

"I thought sure you'd shoot him instead of depending on a slim little rope," said Bob, his heart still pounding like a machine gun.

"Shoot your uncle's thousand-dollar bull!" cried Montana. "He'd likely shoot me if I did."

"D-does one bull cost a thousand dollars?" Bob asked in amazement.

"That one sure does," Montana drawled.

"Whew!" Bob exclaimed. Then after a moment he said

ADVENTURE ON THE RANGE

more seriously, "I'm certainly glad you happened along just then, Montana. You saved my life."

"I reckon I did," Montana answered in a matter-of-fact manner, as if saving lives were an everyday occurrence to him. "But if it hadn't been for old Buttercup, the bull, I maybe never would have found you. I heard him snorting and carrying on, so I knew he was up to some mischief!" Then he asked curiously, "How come you got lost?"

Bob explained.

"I didn't think riding around the barnyard would satisfy you long," Montana said shortly, but there was no smile on his face and his tone was distinctly cool. "But you'd better start learning how to be a cowboy before you start acting like one."

Bob's spirits sank at Montana's tone and manner.

"I'm beginning to see that there is a lot to being a cowboy besides just wearing fancy clothes and riding a galloping horse," Bob admitted. Then he added thoughtfully, "But how am I going to learn to be a real one?"

Montana shrugged. "That *is* a problem," he said as he urged the pony to an easy lope. "Especially now. I reckon it'll be a long time before your uncle lets you on a hoss again."

"I reckon it will," echoed Bob glumly.

Montana tightened the reins and reached for his six-shooter. "Don't jump," he said. "I'm going to fire into the air three times to signal the other fellows that I've found you."

"Oh," said Bob faintly. "D-did all the men go to look for me?"

"Yes," said the foreman after he had fired. "When Calico came to the barn all covered with foam and with the saddle askew, we figured that he had run away with you and thrown you, or that something had happened."

"You don't suppose my uncle will send me home, do you?" Bob asked Montana.

Montana shrugged. "I reckon he is considerable put out," he said shortly.

Bob gulped hard. He grew sick at the thought that he might be sent home now, before he even got a chance to begin being a cowboy.

Montana and Bob were the first ones to reach the house. Cookie was the only one there.

"The only reason Cookie didn't get on a horse to join the search is that he's too fat," Montana told Bob. "There isn't a horse strong enough to bear him up!"

But Cookie didn't laugh. He didn't even smile. He just went on stirring the mess of beans he was cooking in a big kettle.

Bob's heart sank still more. If this was the way Cookie felt, how about the other men? And how about his uncle?

At length Crowbait and Shorty came in, hungry and out of sorts. Bob brought hot water from the kitchen and filled the washbasins on the back porch, but except for a brief thanks the men had nothing to say to him.

Bob sat down at the long table with them. He tried to eat, but in spite of his hunger nothing tasted like food and he had trouble swallowing. The men were silent and gruff and did not even look in his direction.

"W-where's my uncle?" Bob finally managed to blurt out.

Everyone looked at him then, but there was no friendliness in their glances.

"I reckon he's still out looking for a dumb tenderfoot kid that didn't have sense enough to do as he was told," said Crowbait.

Bob felt the crimson mount to his cheeks. He almost choked over the mouthful of food he was trying to swallow. Everyone bent over his plate, and nothing more was said until Montana put in, "I'll signal again when I'm finished here. I reckon the boss didn't hear my first shots."

After the men were through eating, Montana went outside and fired his six-shooter into the air three times. And after a brief interval he signalled again. "I reckon that's about all we can do now," he said. "We might as well amble over to the bunkhouse."

The men stalked off to the bunkhouse, their high-heeled boots clop-clopping on the hard earth.

Bob wandered around aimlessly, wondering what to do with himself. It was dark outside now. Shep was tired and refused to comfort him. Button was nowhere to be found. In desperate need of companionship Bob strolled over to the bunkhouse and stood at the door, looking in. No one invited him to come in or paid the slightest attention to him, not even Montana. Finally he found courage to open the screen door and sidle into the room. Still no one noticed him. Even so, this was better than being by himself in the big ranch house.

When the men began yawning and saying that they had "better hit the hay," there was nothing for Bob to do but go. But before he left he asked, "Isn't anyone going to do anything about my uncle?"

The men looked at him coldly.

"We can't do anything till morning," Crowbait answered. "As it is, we've lost a day's work."

Again the painful flush rose to Bob's cheeks.

Montana took pity on him. "I reckon the old man can take care of himself," he said. "He grew up on this range. Knows it like his hand. I wouldn't worry about him too much. Come morning we'll see what we can see. You just go to sleep now."

Bob went with lagging steps to the log house. It

68

seemed unbearably big and empty and lonesome. The kerosene lamp threw a pool of light in the center of his bedroom but left the rest of the room in weird shadows. Hurriedly he undressed and blew out the light, glad to be rid of those ghostly shapes.

For a long time he lay there drawn into a ball, his ears strained for the sound of hoofbeats. If only his uncle would get back soon, safe and sound, Bob thought, he would be glad to face the punishment that he felt sure was in store for him. But there were no hoofbeats. Only the croak of frogs and the chirp of crickets and the mysterious barnyard noises, and now and again the haunting, far-off howl of a coyote.

It seemed to Bob that he did not miss a sound all that night. But when he went to breakfast in the morning, there sat his uncle at the head of the table.

Bob blinked and gasped. "When did you get back?" he blurted.

His uncle looked at him coldly. "During the night," he said, and that was all. He went on talking to Shorty and paid no more attention to his nephew.

Bob slid into his place and tried to eat, but everything was as tasteless as straw. His heart, which had given a great leap of joy at the sight of his uncle, sank back to the soles of his shoes. Uppermost in his mind now was the dread of what his punishment was to be. He could stand anything except to be sent back home in disgrace. More than ever now he was filled with the desire to prove himself possessed of the qualities that made a real cowboy.

Breakfast over, Bob waited for a chance to speak to his uncle. As soon as they were alone, he stepped up bravely in spite of the rapid beating of his heart.

"I'm awfully sorry about yesterday," he said. "I didn't mean to make such a nuisance of myself. I know I shouldn't have gone out of the yard. I won't do such a thing again."

His uncle looked down at him. For a long moment he did not speak. Then he said, "I'm glad you're man enough to apologize, Bob. You must understand that this is a busy cattle ranch. Anything that causes delay is costly to us. If you can't be helpful, you must at least not make us lose time."

Bob shuffled his feet at the remembrance of neglected chores added to his greater misdeed.

"Also," his uncle went on, "you not only risked your own safety, but you endangered valuable ranch property. Fortunately Calico got back here safely, but often a horse that runs with dangling reins steps on one and breaks a leg."

"I've learned my lesson," Bob said, looking straight at his uncle. "I promise I won't do a thing like that again."

70

His uncle looked at him earnestly. "I believe maybe you have learned that particular lesson," he agreed. "But perhaps you'll learn it better, and be less likely to make similar mistakes, if you spend some time thinking the matter over. So you'd better stay in your room this morning until dinnertime."

Bob gulped twice, then nodded, turned on his heel, and went to his room.

The morning was beautiful with soft, balmy air. The meadow larks sang and the crickets chirped like mad. It would be hard to have to sit in his room all this lovely morning, but it was as if a great load were suddenly lifted from his heart. A little tune trilled through his head. "I'm not being sent home," it ran. "I'm staying on at the Circle K!"

Nevertheless, time soon began to drag. Bob sat with his chin on his hands and his elbows on the window sill and gazed wistfully toward the corral, where a cloud of dust was rising. The men were breaking horses again today. It would have been fun to sit on the top rail and watch them.

He whistled to Shep. The dog threw a look over his shoulder, but Bob's prison did not appeal to him. He wagged his tail apologetically, then trotted toward the corral. Button, paying no attention to Bob's inviting calls, bounded after Shep.

71

Left alone, Bob did some serious thinking. At last he heard the welcome clang of the iron bar against the triangle, signalling the men to dinner. With a sigh of relief he left his room. He felt as though he had done considerable growing up that long morning.

Bob washed his hands and face at the wash bench with the cowboys, then slid into his place at the long table. It was a comfort to realize that the men were treating him as if nothing had happened. He hoped he was back in their good graces again.

6. A Battle for Mastery

WHEN the men came in to dinner, they were arguing fiercely. At first Bob could not make out what it was about. He could see that Montana was defending himself and that the other men all seemed to have taken sides against him.

"You're so doggoned sure of yourself," Crowbait was saying sarcastically. "You're supposed to be a top hand. You have quite a reputation for hoss sense. I reckon then that you're willing to back up your reputation in this matter by something worth-while."

"You can be sure of that," Montana said positively. "I'll give you my silver-mounted rodeo saddle if I don't ride that hoss."

Bob gasped, then held his breath. He knew that, next to his favorite horse Silver, Montana treasured above all his possessions the handsome saddle he had won as prize in the rodeo the year before. It was a finer saddle than any of the other men owned.

The conversation continued, growing louder and more serious. Still Bob did not discover what it was all about until Montana burst out hotly, "I'll not only ride Dynamite but I'll bust him, too."

At this all the other cowboys broke into loud and jeering laughter.

Shorty, who had seemed to be partly on Montana's side, shook his head at this statement. This was evidently going too far in his opinion.

"Success has gone to his head," Bob heard Shorty say to Uncle John. "He's plumb loco. Thinks there isn't any animal he can't get the best of. Too bad. When a top hand gets that notion, he's headed for the dust. Dynamite will throw him so high the birds'll build nests in his hair before he lights."

"I'm so sure I can bust Dynamite," Montana said calmly, "that I'll throw in Silver along with my saddle if I don't do it." The cowhands gasped. "But this whole thing is pretty one-sided," Montana went on evenly. "I ought to have some sort of prize if I succeed."

"If you break Dynamite," John Benton promised, "I'll give him to you."

"And the rest of us will pitch in," Shorty cried, "and buy you the best pair of cowboy boots Ted Russel can

74

make." The others cheerfully backed up Shorty's offer.

"I'm glad you fellows are making the ride worth my while," Montana drawled. "I'd do it anyway, just for the fun of it, but such fine prizes make it more interesting."

Everyone broke into excited talk. They all agreed that Dynamite was an outlaw horse. One that could never be ridden, much less broken. They also agreed that probably he was a killer.

Bob felt shivers run up and down his spine. He knew that the other men were experienced in the ways of horse nature, too. It did seem that Montana was being pretty reckless to risk his life this way. He felt all tied up in knots of tension. He looked inquiringly toward the head of the table, wondering if his uncle would allow him to go to the corral.

"Go ahead," John Benton nodded, and relief flooded Bob's heart. Evidently nothing more was going to be said about his misadventure of the previous day.

Bob followed the men outside and climbed to the top rail, his heart beating hard.

Montana said nothing as he walked toward the corral. But he strode ahead of the other Circle K hands with the air of self-confidence that Bob admired. Three of the cowboys went to the large corral to cut out Dynamite and force him into the chute that led into the smaller corral where the horses were gentled.

The commotion in the big corral was terriffc. It was evident that the other horses there considered Dynamite a killer, for they squealed with terror and scattered in all directions every time he came their way. And when the maddened animal threw himself, pawing and wild eyed, against the sides of the corral, Bob wondered if the poles would hold.

Montana was saving his energy for the great contest ahead. He sat on the top rail and laughed at the perspiring cowboys who were trying to get Dynamite into the small corral.

"I reckon I'll have to come and help you," he drawled.

"Save your steam," Crowbait puffed. "You're going to need every ounce of it or I'm a spavined hunk o' hoss meat."

"I reckon you are," Montana grinned. "But do get a move on. I'm getting bored with this inaction."

"You won't be that way long," Shorty called to him, as Dynamite was finally cornered in the narrow chute between the corrals and the gate dropped behind him.

When the horse found himself imprisoned, he went crazier than ever. He squealed and battered the poles with his forefeet until Bob could feel the corral tremble. Then Shorty swung the gate leading from the chute into the small corral, and Dynamite came into it like a ton of his namesake.

76

Dynamite came in
like a ton of his namesake

Bob involuntarily drew up his legs as the enraged animal came his way. But Montana only continued to gaze at the horse with quiet amusement.

"A hoss with that much spirit will be a good animal after I take the spook out of him," he drawled.

"Huh!" grunted Crowbait, who was now sitting on the top rail beside Bob. "You're as crazy as popcorn on a hot stove. Ice will melt at the North Pole before you get the spook out of that boy. He's a killer or I never saw one."

Bob glanced quickly up at Montana and was surprised to see a look of tenseness on the foreman's face in spite of the grin. In a flood of understanding it came to him how much this contest meant to his friend. It meant not only his most prized possessions—his fine horse (and Bob knew that a cowboy's horses were like members of his family) and his saddle, the finest in the whole range country—but he was also staking his reputation as the best horsebreaker in the country. And perhaps, Bob thought with a sudden start, he was even staking his life.

"What are you waiting for?" Crowbait called, a jeering grin on his face. "Ain't scared, are you?"

"Scared of that amiable creature?" Montana drawled. "Naw. I've just got to give my dinner a little time to digest before I let him begin tossing it around."

"Huh, you're hoping he'll get himself all worn out," Crowbait scoffed.

Bob didn't like the tone of Crowbait's remarks. The cowboys, although they teased each other constantly, were usually good-natured about it. But there was always an undercurrent of meanness in Crowbait's teasing remarks to Montana. Bob wondered again if Crowbait envied Montana's top ranking in the Circle K.

But Montana paid no attention to Crowbait. Deliberately, he untangled his long legs from the top rail, jumped down into the corral, and commenced to twirl his rope.

At sight of this hated, two-legged enemy, Dynamite stopped his wild prancings. Then, with a squeal of fury, he threw himself at the man, rearing high into the air, forelegs pawing. At the same time Montana's rope snaked out.

Bob almost stopped breathing. Would his friend waste his loop and not have time to form another before those sharp hoofs would be upon him?

But miraculously the loop settled neatly around Dynamite's neck. Quick as a thought, Montana wrapped the other end around the snubbing post. His high heels plowed the dirt as he tightened the noose that was choking the meanness out of the horse. Then he yelled for someone to bring a blindfold and for someone else to hold the end of the rope while he lifted the saddle to throw on Dynamite's back.

79

"Well, I'm a spavined hunk o' hoss meat," cried Crowbait. "If he don't aim to ride that ornery animal without trying to gentle it first!"

And that did seem to be Montana's aim—to get along without any of the usual preliminary motions of letting the animal become accustomed to the man smell or to the feel of first the blanket, then the saddle, on his back. Swiftly Montana threw the saddle blanket on, then the saddle. Then, while Shorty and Crowbait twisted the animal's ears and held the blindfold in place, he leaped into the saddle. Crowbait jerked the blindfold and along with Shorty clambered to the top of the fence.

For a moment the horse stood still as though unable to believe that the weight on his back was real. Then he exploded all over the corral.

"Jumping Jimminy!" Shorty exclaimed. "He has all the mean tricks of all the mean hosses I ever saw rolled into that ornery carcass of his. He can wrinkle his spine, high-roll, weave, sunfish, swap ends, jackknife, and everything else."

Bob did not see how any human being could remain seated on the leaping, twisting animal. Most of the time Dynamite's back formed a peak in the middle and his head was between his forelegs. Time and again he swapped ends, as Shorty called it, so suddenly that it seemed a miracle that Montana stuck in the saddle. He had a dozen different motions of the terrific, jerky sort that make a talented bucker.

"I'm beginning to wish we hadn't started this," Shorty gasped. "I'm too fond of Montana for this sort of thing."

"But Montana's riding him!" Bob cried. His hands gripped the top pole of the corral until his knuckles showed white. He ached all over, outside and in, with his concern for his friend and the intensity of his desire to have him triumph.

Shorty shook his head soberly. "That ornery devil hasn't used up all of his tricks yet," he said. "If he does throw Montana, he'll likely paw him to death before the fellow can get up. Or he's likely to start rolling if he can't get rid of him any other way." The cowhand drew a long sigh. "As for me," he concluded, "I'm willing to call it a day. But it's too late now. Montana's got to ride, or else . . ."

Bob gripped the rail and breathed a silent prayer. "Oh, stick on, Montana! Stick on!"

Around and around the corral they went. The spectators were silent now, lost in admiration for both horse and rider. They had been witnessing daring and skillful riding for most of their lives, but never had they seen anything like this. And never had they seen so tireless a horse. Long before this time an ordinary horse would have collapsed. Dynamite was covered with foam and

81

at every leap his breath was forced from him with an agonized grunt, yet he would not give up. But finally the leaps became less wild and at last the horse's head came up. This, Shorty explained to Bob, was a sign that the bucking was over, for a horse cannot buck unless its head is between its legs.

Montana slid to the ground. Instantly Crowbait snatched the saddle and bridle from the horse, before it could find energy for more tricks.

Everyone slapped Montana on the back as he walked toward the bunkhouse. Even Crowbait seemed sincere in his admiration over the ride. And that night at supper no one could talk of anything else.

"You won your prize with interest," John Benton said. "That ride was worth a lot. What do you say, men? Has Montana earned the right to keep his saddle and his cow pony?"

The men gladly agreed with Mr. Benton's generous suggestion. Bob heaved a sigh of relief. Montana certainly should not be required to do any more, to risk his life again after such a wonderful ride. Perhaps luck would not be with him another time. Besides everyone believed that it was impossible to break Dynamite.

Montana looked up from his plate. "What's the matter?" he asked coolly. "Are you men trying to back out of your offers?"

"No," said Shorty. "It isn't that, and you know it. We're only trying to do the square thing by you. We know and you know that you can't break Dynamite. We don't hanker to have you risk your hide, trying a fool stunt like that."

"You've never known me to back out of anything, have you?" Montana asked.

"No," cried Shorty in exasperation. "And you aren't backing out now. We're asking you as a favor to us not to risk your fool neck again. We're shorthanded on the Circle K as it is. We can't spare any top hands."

"I made a proposition and I'll stick to it," said Montana quietly. "Either I'll break Dynamite in a week's time or you fellows get my saddle and my cow pony."

The men shrugged and went on with their eating. Bob wished that Montana would not be so stubborn. Oh, why wouldn't he quit now!

"You'll have to break Dynamite on your own time, Montana," Bob's uncle said. "I'm inclined to agree with Shorty and the other boys that there's an unbreakable horse. I don't think he's worth taking time to work with. I planned to save him for a rodeo horse. But if you want to work with him in your spare time that's your business."

"I reckon he'll be the top hoss in my string one of these days," said Montana with a broad grin.

"Don't go countin' your hosses until they are broke," Crowbait warned.

That night Bob took his flashlight and wandered out to the breaking corral. Dynamite was to stay there until the end of the week, because the cowboys had refused to risk their necks cutting him out from the cavy and getting him into the chute again.

At the sound of Bob's footsteps Dynamite let out a fierce whinny. Bob heard his hoofs hit the poles. "Steady, boy, steady," he said soothingly.

"Steady, boy, yourself," he heard, and jumped at the sound.

"What do you think you're doing out here all by your lonesome?"

Bob recognized Montana's familiar voice. "Oh," he laughed, "you scared me more than the horse did! I just came out to talk to Dynamite a little. I thought it might help you if I talked to him a bit and sort of got him used to people."

"Thanks, pal." Montana chuckled. "You have the makings of a real cowboy. You and I had the same idea. Climb up here to the 'opery rail' and we'll have a little powwow and let Dynamite in on it."

Bob perched beside his friend contentedly.

"You know," Montana went on, "I believe he is beginning to understand already that we're meant to be friends."

But if Dynamite had such an understanding, he was very backward about showing it. For two days the men watched Montana each time he gave Dynamite his workout, then they tired of it. By now the horse was able to throw his rider once in a while. He had the advantage of not getting worn out in the battle of changing corrals and he was bursting with energy. But Montana was as agile as a panther. Almost as soon as he hit the ground he was on his feet and back in the saddle again, letting Dynamite feel the bite of the spurs after each victory. Finally the horse began to understand that the short triumph was hardly worth the punishment.

Only Bob knew that Montana went out every night and worked with Dynamite. Talking to him soothingly. Roping and tying him to the snubbing post. Rubbing his neck. Letting him wear the saddle for an hour at a time.

When the night before the end of the week came, Montana said to Bob, "S'pose you can get up before daylight tomorrow?"

"I reckon I can," said Bob, who would have slept standing on his head if Montana had requested it. "Why?"

"Well, I aim to get up before the birdies myself," Montana drawled. "Tomorrow is the day for me to collect my prize. So I want to give friend Dynamite here a bit of a workout before the sun rises. Take some of the spook out of him before the boys are up. When they come out, I want you to open the gate so I can come riding out on a hoss with his head up."

"I'll sure do that," Bob told him with delight.

That night Bob set his alarm for three o'clock, the time when Montana said he was going to begin the workout. Dynamite had never given up bucking whenever Montana first got into the saddle. But now it was more like the game of a mischievous child than the determined meanness of a killer horse.

Bob had seen Montana ride Dynamite around the corral after several of his bucking sprees. The horse acted promising enough then, but Montana had not yet attempted to ride him out in the open. After all, that would be the test. Dynamite might have learned the uselessness of fighting his heart out in the prison of the corral, but when he saw the wide open spaces the urge for freedom might prove to be stronger than the brief mastery Montana had managed to attain.

It was with considerable uneasiness the next morning that Bob called down to his friend, from his lookout on

86

the top of the corral, that the men were coming from the bunkhouse.

"Open the gate then," Montana called, "and keep your fingers crossed, pal."

Dynamite stepped between the poles of the gate with head high and ears perked up.

"Steady, boy, steady!" Montana said quietly, his hand firm on the rein. Dynamite jerked his head as though in an attempt to get the bit between strong teeth, but Montana was prepared for just such a trick.

"No you don't, boy," he said. "Just remember that I'm boss, and we'll get along fine."

The spirited animal made two more attempts to bolt for the beckoning freedom of green meadows and blue hills. But the grip on the reins remained firm and the suggestion of spur against flank reminded him that the two-legged creature astride him was still determined to be master.

Bob held his breath. Would Dynamite bog his head and use his tremendous energy to rid himself of the burden on his back? There was plenty of room for the horse to put his strength to the test if he happened to take the notion.

But the horse trotted around the buildings with beautifully arched neck and high steps.

The men stood speechless, their mouths open with

amazement. Cookie came out to whang the triangle and froze midway in the motion. John Benton appeared at the door, half his face clean-shaven, the rest covered with lather.

No one said a word as the handsome horse continued to high-step around the yard. Bob's heart, however, was still in his throat, for Dynamite's nostrils were dilated and he threw walleyed glances about.

Montana was the only one who seemed undisturbed. "How do you like my new hoss?" he called as he trotted by the men. "Isn't he a handsome brute? Don't you wish you had one as good?"

"Well I'll be a hornswoggled hunk o' hoss meat," Shorty cried. "If Montana didn't go and do it again. I never saw his like!"

Several times Dynamite tried to get his head down, but the alert, strong hand on the reins reminded him who was master.

After riding around the buildings for several minutes, Montana signalled Bob to open the corral gate. The foreman rode inside and removed the saddle.

As he came out, John Benton called, "That's a splendid new horse you have there, Montana."

The cowboy grinned. "I reckon he is," he drawled. "And my silver-trimmed saddle will look mighty fine on him."

"Right today," Shorty promised, "we'll get the order off for those new boots. You've really earned them."

"He sure has," the other cowboys echoed.

Bob looked down at his brown oxfords. "I wish I could do something to win a pair of cowboy boots," he thought. Then quickly forgot his desire in his joy over Montana's triumph.

7. A Horse to Gentle

THE MORNING after Montana's famous ride, Mr. Benton spoke up at the breakfast table. "Don't forget, boys," he said, "the west fence has to be ridden and repaired today."

The men looked at one another.

"I know what you're thinking," Uncle John said in his crisp tones. "None of you wants this job of fence-riding and repairing the wire. I hate to ask good cowmen like you to do such a job, but you know we're so shorthanded that we have to double up on work."

Bob had been on the ranch long enough now to know that the cowboys considered beneath them anything that must be done afoot. So long as a cowboy was astride a horse he felt he was king of all he surveyed. Bob himself had got a little taste of that feeling the time he had galloped wild and free toward the blue mountains. Since a man could scarcely repair a broken fence astride a horse, this was a job none of the cowboys cared for.

"Suppose you draw lots to see who gets the job of line-rider," Mr. Benton suggested.

To Bob's disappointment, Montana got the short broomstraw.

"May I go along and help?" Bob asked. "I wouldn't mind mending fences. I can drive nails."

Montana looked at the boss questioningly. "How about it?" he asked. "I'll pick the kid a gentle hoss and look after him. I reckon he would be quite helpful."

"All right," Mr. Benton agreed. "So long as you will be with him to look out for him. But remember," he told Bob, "Montana has work to do. You mustn't be in the way."

Bob felt his face turn red. He did wish Uncle John wouldn't treat him like a three-year-old. He knew that he could be of some use on the ranch if only his uncle would give him the chance.

But the sting of his uncle's words was lessened by Montana's quick remark, "Oh, Bob here is my right-hand man. I really need him."

Montana soon brought in three horses from the cavy. One he was to ride himself. One, called "Peanuts," Bob was to ride. The third was a pack horse that was to carry equipment for mending fences.

"I saddled your hoss for you this time," Montana told Bob as they set out. "But if you're to be a cowboy you must learn to saddle and take care of your own pony. That's the first thing a cowman learns to do—take care of his animal. A waddy that won't do that isn't worth his salt."

Bob nodded his head. "When a new man comes to the ranch to ask for a job," Montana went on, "we always look over his hoss before we take him on. If there are saddle marks or spur scars, or if the hoss looks underfed, that hombre is sent on his way pronto. Your uncle wouldn't have him on the place."

"I want to learn to saddle and take care of a horse," said Bob seriously. "Because I want to be a real cowboy—a top hand—someday. But the trouble is, my uncle seems to think I'm only about three years old instead of twelve. He's afraid I'll get hurt or something. He won't let me start being a cowboy."

"I've noticed that," Montana said understandingly. "The thing to do is to prove to your uncle somehow that you're old enough and dependable enough to start being a cowboy."

"I wish I could!" Bob cried.

"He naturally doesn't want anything to happen to you," Montana continued. "And of course a cowboy's life is full of danger. You can't get away from that."

"I know," Bob agreed. "Cowboys have to be awfully brave. I went to the movies at home every time there was a western picture. I think it's awfully exciting the way cowboys are always riding galloping horses and rescuing people and things like that."

Montana grinned. "Well, life on a cattle ranch isn't always exactly the way the movie people show it. We don't ride our hosses at full gallop all the time for one thing. Real cowboys don't mistreat their ponies that way. And we don't go around singing everywhere and we aren't always rescuing people. But there's plenty of excitement. I wouldn't live any other kind of life if I had a million dollars."

Bob found that fence-riding was not very exciting. He and Montana rode along the barbed-wire fence, examining it. Whenever they found a place that had come loose from the posts, Montana let Bob dismount and drive in the staples to fasten it tight. But when they found a place where the wires were actually broken, Montana got off his horse and repaired the break.

Bob knew that when the men left the ranch house for work of this kind they went without lunch. When the sun got high overhead, he was almost famished. But he said nothing; he was doing a cowboy's job.

It was not all work. Whenever they came to a long stretch, they would gallop a bit. Montana showed Bob

93

how to bear his weight in the stirrups, how to allow his body to give with the motion of the horse, how to hold the reins.

"You catch on fast," the top hand said approvingly. "You have the makings of a good rider."

Bob's eyes sparkled at this praise from Montana. "I just wish I had a horse of my own," he said. "I used to

The yearling

want cowboy boots more than anything in the world. I still want them. But now I want a horse more. Sometimes at night I dream about having a pony of my own."

"I know just how you feel," Montana said. "I used to feel that way, too, when I was a kid." He drew up his pony and pointed to a small group of horses in a fenced meadow. "See that yearling colt over there? The bay with the star on its forehead and the three white feet."

Bob nodded. He had no trouble picking out the one that Montana meant. Even to his inexperienced eyes that colt had something special about it. "It's the best-looking colt I ever saw!" he cried.

Montana nodded. "You're getting to be a good judge of hoss flesh. Well, I happen to be part owner of that colt. That is, the mare that mothered it belongs to me. Its father belongs to your uncle. It's rather inconvenient to own just half a colt," he grinned. "Someday I hope to make a deal with the boss. But anyway, long as the colt is half mine, I'll let you help me take care of my half of it. And if you can manage to help gentle it and train it, why maybe next summer you'll have a young hoss to ride."

Bob's heart almost stopped beating with excitement.

"Mind, I'm not saying you can have it for your own," Montana put in quickly. "It isn't mine to give. And besides, folks don't just go around giving away valuable

95

hosses. But it's time the colt began its training, and it would do you good to have something to tame. Of course, it isn't old enough to be ridden or used as a cow pony."

"Of course not," Bob agreed. "But if I could help train it, it would seem like mine! And maybe Dad and Mother would let me come here again next summer, and you would let me ride it—!"

"It all depends on how good you are at training it," Montana said. "I wouldn't let you ride even your uncle's half unless you proved yourself able to handle good hoss flesh."

As they jogged back to the main ranch, Bob was lost in a daze of pleasant daydreams of training and riding the little bay with the three white feet.

8. The Shindig

THE FOLLOWING SATURDAY MORNING Bob noticed that the Circle K cowboys plunged into their work with unusual vigor. That night there was to be a big "shindig" at the neighboring Flying V Ranch. During breakfast the men could talk of nothing else. They gulped down hot cakes, bacon and eggs, and scalding coffee, eager to get at their day's work and finish it in ample time to slick up for the occasion.

"What is a shindig?" Bob asked.

"You don't know what a shindig is?" Crowbait asked in amazement. And all the men looked shocked at such ignorance.

"I never heard of such a thing," Bob confessed.

Finally Montana took pity on him. "A shindig is—well, it's just a shindig," he said lamely. "A big hoedown. A get-together. Everyone comes from miles around. Some fellows bring their fiddles. Happy, here, will take his guitar. They play music for the square dances. The ladies and gals bring sandwiches and cakes and pies. And everyone has a high old time."

"It sounds like fun!" Bob turned to his uncle. "May I go to the shindig, Uncle John?" he asked eagerly.

John Benton pursed his lips and studied the matter for a long moment. He seemed to be on the point of refusing. Bob held his breath.

"He can go in the 'pickup' with me," Happy offered. "I'll keep my eye on him."

"We-ll," the words came out slowly. "I believe he can go. I don't see how any harm can come to him."

"Oh, thanks!" Bob exclaimed.

Supper was a hurried affair that night, with much talk and banter about the shindig. Bob never had seen the men spend so much time cleaning themselves up. They polished their boots, doused oil on their hair, and put on their brightest silk shirts and neckerchiefs.

Most of the men rode horseback to the Flying V, but Happy drove the pickup because he was to take some of the food. Bob saw him wrap his guitar case tenderly in a blanket before he carefully tucked it into the car.

"Aren't you going to the shindig?" Bob asked his uncle.

"No, I'm afraid my dancing days are over," Mr. Benton said. "Someone has to stay at the ranch, and the job suits me very well. Have a good time, Bob. When you get tired you can go out and sleep in the pickup. The boys always stay until morning."

Cookie rode with Bob and Happy. As they spun along, he and Happy told Bob that the Flying V was a dude ranch that made a business of entertaining city people who wanted a taste of ranch life without any of the hardships. Bob noticed a touch of contempt in their tone as they spoke of the Flying V hands as "dude wranglers."

When they got to the big barn where the dance was being held, the place was a gay sight. Electrically-wired lanterns hung from the rafters and bales of hay had been placed along the walls for seats. Bob was amused to see that the dude wranglers were dressed much like the cowboys he had seen in the movies. They wore bright-colored, braid-trimmed silk shirts, brighter neckerchiefs, and tight-fitting trousers trimmed with braid. Their hats were extra wide with fancy bands, and some of them wore chaps decorated with large silver conchas. Most of the dudes were also fixed up in fancy western clothes.

"Howdy, stranger!" A voice beside him made Bob start. He turned to look into the most thoroughly freckled face he had ever seen, on a boy about his own age.

99

"Oh, howdy!" Bob returned, smiling.

"I'm Jerry Bates. I live on the ranch just north of your uncle's," the freckled boy said with a friendly grin. "I hear you're spending the summer on the Circle K. Why don't you ride over sometime?"

Bob gulped and felt his face turn red. He didn't want to admit that he wasn't allowed to ride outside the ranch.

"Oh, I don't know my way around very well yet," he finally found words. "Why don't you ride over to the Circle K?"

"I might do that," Jerry answered.

The two boys stood watching the square dancers. Bob had never seen dancing like this before. The cowboys entered into the spirit of the thing with little restraint and considerable hilarity. The "caller" stood on a chair and bellowed directions:

> All jump up and never come down,
> Swing your honey around and around
> Till the hollow of your foot
> Makes a hole in the ground.
>   And promenade! Oh, promenade!

> Rope your cow and brand your calf,
> Swing your honey a loop and a half.
> Come on now with the old mess wagon,
> Hind wheel's broke and the axle's draggin'.
>   Swing, swing! Everybody swing!

The cowboys stamped and whooped to liven things up. Bob noticed that Shorty was the liveliest and noisiest of them all. "He's one of our men," Bob laughed, pointing him out.

"He's really having a good time," Jerry observed.

Happy strummed his guitar

Bob watched Montana, whirling around gracefully in the most intricate figures of the square dances. It seemed only natural to him that the foreman should excel at everything he did. And he noticed that, although most of the musicians smiled and stamped their feet as they played, Happy strummed his guitar with as dead seriousness as he did everything else.

101

The girls and women from the neighboring ranches wore silk, rather frilly dresses, but the "dudines," the women and girls staying at the dude ranch, wore Levis (overalls) or riding breeches and brightly checked shirts.

There were about three times as many men as ladies, but the cowboys were not to be left without partners. Some of them tied handkerchiefs about their arms to indicate that they were ladies. "They call that 'heifer-branding' the cowboys," Jerry explained.

He and Bob laughed to see the other cowboys bow and scrape and go through all sorts of ridiculous antics for the privilege of dancing with these simpering creatures. The boys almost doubled up as they watched Cookie, who was one of the "ladies." "She" turned out to be the belle of the ball, rolling "her" eyes in a most flirtatious manner and walking with mincing steps that contrasted ridiculously with "her" ponderous weight.

As the two boys wandered around the great barn, Bob was surprised to see in one corner a dozen or more babies and small children, fast asleep on hard benches.

"I don't see how they do it," he said—"sleep with all this music and whooping and laughing going on!"

"I don't either," Jerry laughed, "but I used to do it myself. My folks began to drag me to these shindigs when I was only knee high to a grasshopper. So I practically grew up sleeping in places like this."

Bob stared down at the small children lying there. "Ever hear how some cowpokes switched babies at one of these dances?" Jerry asked.

"No. Tell me about it."

"It really happened not very far from here," Jerry said. "My father read me the story out of a book called *The Virginian*. They had all the babies asleep in one of the bedrooms, and these fellows went in and changed the babies around. There was quite a mix-up when their mamas went to get them."

Bob laughed.

Jerry looked thoughtful for a moment. Then he whispered, "I have an idea. A humdinger!" He seized Bob's arm. "Come along with me."

Bob followed him outside. Near the barn there was a long rail to which the cowboys' horses were tied.

"We'll switch the ponies," whispered Jerry. "It's so dark out here the fellows can't see their animals, so each cowboy will just come to where he tied his pony and climb on without thinking. They dance till nearly daylight and by then the men are so dead tired they generally go to sleep while they're riding. They depend on their ponies to take them home."

Bob put his hand over his mouth to keep back a shout of mirth. "Most of the cowboys will wake up on some other ranch—not their own," he whispered.

"Yeh," Jerry chuckled. "Each pony will go to his home ranch. There'll be an awful mix-up of cowboys in the morning."

"This is a better joke than mixing up the babies," Bob said, in deep admiration over Jerry's genius. "This really should be in a book, too."

Bob settled himself cozily between Happy and Cookie as the shindig broke up in that dark hour just before dawn. Everyone was groggy with weariness and yawning widely as good nights were said.

Bob chuckled as he thought of the mixed-up horses.

"What's funny, partner?" Cookie asked.

"Oh, I just happened to think of something," Bob answered briefly.

Happy started to sing in a sleepy voice one of his favorite songs:

> Oh, give me a home where the buffalo roam,
> Where the deer and the antelope play,
> Where seldom is heard a discouraging word
> And the skies are not cloudy all day.

Bob, lulled by Happy's singing, promptly went to sleep, to be awakened by Cookie's booming voice, "Here we are back on the home range. Wake up, Bob!"

As Bob climbed stiffly from the pickup, Happy said mournfully, "There won't be time for any snoozing at

*Bob and Jerry
switched the ponies*

all. When we have one of these all-night shindigs, we might as well count it a night's sleep lost and let it go at that."

"Then why don't people go home earlier?" Bob asked a trifle crossly. "Why do they stay all night?"

"Oh, we cowmen don't have many social events," Happy yawned. "So when we do, we have to make the most of it." He looked toward the eastern sky which the dawn was beginning to tinge with pink. "Just in time to get in the hosses," he added dolefully.

"And Bob and I are just in time to get breakfast," said Cookie, as spryly as if he had had a full night's sleep. "Shake a leg there, partner, and get the wood and water in and set the places at the table."

Bob's feet dragged as he did his chores, though the smell of cooking bacon and coffee revived him a bit. He heard some of the men coming in, shouting at one another across the barnyard as cheerfully as though they were not tired at all.

As Bob slid sleepily into his place at the table, he suddenly remembered something. He looked about quickly. Then he gasped. He had taken pains to see that Crowbait's horse was changed, but there sat Crowbait, eating as though nothing unpleasant had ever happened to him. It was Montana who was missing! No one had seen him since the party.

106

"It's possible he might have got his hoss mixed up," Crowbait remarked, and Bob thought he felt a glance in his direction. "I noticed my pony was tied in a different place. Might be, the animals got tired of standing in the same spot and moved about just for fun. I was smart enough to notice. Probably a dumb guy like Montana wouldn't."

Almost as Crowbait spoke, Montana dragged himself into the room. He smiled rather sheepishly, but he looked half-dead with weariness.

A mighty guffaw of laughter greeted him.

Suddenly Bob didn't think the trick was clever at all. If it had been Crowbait who had made the useless ride to some far-away ranch, he wouldn't have minded. But not for anything would he have pulled a trick like this on his friend Montana.

"It's a wise man that knows his own hoss. Especially after a dance." Crowbait laughed in the disagreeable manner he had. "Me, I had sense enough to notice whether I was mounted on my own animal."

Montana grinned wearily. "I reckon I deserve your kidding," he said. "Any cowpoke that don't recognize his own hoss, even in the dark and when he's half asleep, deserves a lot of kidding. I'm just too unsuspecting, I reckon. But I never thought anyone would pull a skunky trick like that."

107

He looked straight at Crowbait, and his eyes were like cold steel.

"Don't look at me," Crowbait shrugged. "Why don't you ask Bob if he knows anything about it?"

All eyes turned on Bob.

"You—of all people?" Montana cried.

Bob wished the floor would swallow him.

Montana said nothing more. He sat down and piled hot cakes on his plate. Everyone else went on eating.

When the men went outside, Bob tagged along after Montana. The cowboy paid no attention. Finally Bob plucked him by the sleeve.

"Sa-ay," he blurted, "I'm sure sorry about what I did last night. Changing horses, I mean—"

"Whose idea was it?" Montana asked sharply.

"It was Jerry's, really," Bob admitted. "But I thought it was awfully good. That is, at first I did. But I didn't mean to play such a trick on *you*."

"O.K.," Montana said, and the old familiar grin came back to his face. "I've pulled too many tricks on other fellows to hold any grudge when I'm the victim. I reckon I can take a joke as well as play one."

Something welled up in Bob's heart that made it actually hurt. Gee, but Montana was a swell guy!

108

9. Riding on the Roundup

"I've got a surprise for you, partner," Montana said to
Bob one day the next week. "I persuaded your uncle to
let you ride with me on the calf roundup tomorrow."

"Me? Ride with you?" Bob could hardly believe his
ears.

"Yep. I need a right-hand helper. Someone who isn't
afraid. Who will take orders and do what I say pronto."
Montana looked at Bob out of the corner of his eyes.
"And who won't whine or complain, no matter how tired
he feels."

"That's me," Bob cried. "Golly! If I can go on the calf
roundup with you I won't whine or complain ever. In
fact, I won't even get tired."

"We'll see about that." Montana grinned. "You'll have
to go without lunch, you know, and it won't be any picnic. It will be hard work from daylight to dark."

109

"Are you trying to scare me?" Bob laughed. "Riding on the roundup will be fun."

"You'll find out," Montana said darkly. "But I like your spirit. Only don't bog down on me in the middle of the day. If you're going to be my partner, you'll have to stick with me till we are finished."

"I won't bog down," Bob promised. Then he asked, "What is a calf roundup anyway?"

"We have to gather in the calves that haven't been branded," Montana told him.

"Gee whillikers!" cried Bob, his eyes sparkling with excitement. "I'm sure glad I'm going to help with the roundup and branding. I'll be a regular cowboy then!"

"That remains to be seen." Montana's eyes twinkled. "Tomorrow night I can tell whether you're a real cowboy or not."

Bob rushed through his chores the next morning, then trotted along at Montana's heels.

"You can ride Peanuts," the foreman said. "And there's the saddle you can use. I think the stirrups are about right for you."

Bob lifted the saddle from the rail. Peanuts glanced over his shoulder, as if aware that an amateur was at work, and switched his tail and swelled up in the middle. Bob put one foot against the pony's side, as he had seen the men do, to help pull the cinch.

Some of the cowboys were already mounted. Their horses were bucking and plunging mischievously, as they usually did early in the morning, before the "snorts" had been taken out of them. Bob hoped that his horse wouldn't buck. He pulled himself up in the saddle and kept hold of the pommel, prepared for a bit of plunging if it came. Peanuts did commence a few stiff-legged crowhops, and then the unexpected happened. The saddle turned, and Bob found himself, head down, underneath the pony.

Peanuts was evidently even more startled than his rider. Too startled, in fact, to do more than stop in his tracks, spraddle his front legs and lower his head to stare with amazement at this creature hanging beneath his belly.

In a moment Bob recovered his senses enough to kick his feet loose from the stirrups and pick himself up. As he stood on his feet again, he wondered why no one had come to help him. The men were bursting into great guffaws of laughter and slapping their thighs. Bob tried to laugh, too, but it was a feeble attempt.

Montana walked up and twisted the saddle onto Peanut's back. He pulled on the girth until the horse grunted and was forced to suck in his breath.

"Hop on now," Montana told Bob. "And handle the reins so this ornery hoss knows you mean to be boss."

111

Bob, angry at having appeared ridiculous in front of the Circle K men, was determined to let the horse know who was master. It almost seemed as if Peanuts sensed what was in the mind of the person astride him, in the way horses have. He crowhopped halfheartedly for a few steps, but at the firm tug on his reins compromised by snorting instead of bucking.

Bob glanced toward Montana and found the cowboy looking at him with approval. His heart gave a leap of pleasure.

The men scattered to the far corners of the ranch, according to a prearranged plan. Most of the cows with calves had already been gathered in the pasture adjoining the branding corral, but there were always some that managed to hide in brush or in the gullies scattered over the many acres.

Shorty and Montana and Bob galloped along side by side.

"You did almost right," Montana told Bob. "You kicked your feet out of the stirrups, and that was exactly right. Only you didn't do it quick enough. Next time you feel your saddle turning, kick your feet loose right away. Usually a hoss will run when the saddle turns underneath it."

"Is that why no one came to help me?" Bob asked.

Montana nodded. "I reckon Peanuts was too surprised

to run. I never saw anything so funny as when he stared between his front legs that way."

Montana and Shorty commenced to laugh again. Bob tried to join them, but his heart was not in it.

"It's really not so funny," Shorty said when he got his breath. "I've known of fellows getting dragged to death. If you get your foot caught in the stirrup when your saddle turns or when you get thrown, you're in a bad fix."

"I'll remember that," Bob said.

"And when a hoss swells up like that when you tighten the girth," Shorty went on, "it'll take more than one tug to get the wind out of him enough to make your saddle stick."

"I'll remember that, too," Bob promised. Then he added thoughtfully, "I can see now what Uncle John meant when he said a person couldn't learn to be a cowboy in a day."

Before that night Bob discovered that it would take a good while to learn all about the orneriness of cow nature. The creatures seemed to have a talent for hiding in out-of-the-way places and in rocky gullies where it was almost impossible to drive them out. By noon he had found what it meant to be weary and exasperated and so hungry that he was sure he could have eaten raw one of the stubborn creatures they were driving. But he made no complaint and he kept his eyes on Montana so that he could tell by his signals what the cowboy wanted, for some of the time they were too widely separated for words to be understood. After a while Bob began to catch on to what was expected of him without being told. The intelligent little animal he was riding helped in this, for Peanuts was experienced in working with cattle and usually knew what to do without much guidance of the neck rein.

In spite of his weariness Bob found it fun. By mid-afternoon he had got a sort of second wind, and the pur-

*Bob grew weary
driving the stubborn creatures*

suit of elusive cattle up hill and down dale and around trees seemed rather like a game.

Montana grinned at him when they came together after chasing one particularly exasperating mama cow and her calf from a dense growth of shrubs.

"I believe you like being a cowboy," he teased, wiping the sweat from his face with his bandanna.

"Oh, I do!" cried Bob. "This is really fun. But I could certainly use something to eat right now."

"Well, s'pose we light and take a big drink of water from this 'crick' instead," Montana suggested.

"That suits me," said Bob. And sliding down he sank to his stomach and placed his lips to the cool stream.

"Whoa, there!" Montana shouted. "Haven't you forgotten something?"

Bob lifted his head. "What?" he asked.

"Your reins. Do you want to be left afoot a good dozen miles from home?"

"Oh!" cried Bob, getting up and trailing on the ground the reins he had left wrapped around the saddle horn.

"I thought you knew that if you leave the reins up, your hoss is likely to high-tail it for home," Montana said accusingly. "Ranch hosses are trained to stand when the reins are left tied to the ground."

"I did know that," Bob said apologetically. "I forgot. I won't do it again."

"Oh, you'll learn," Montana encouraged him. "I notice that you're getting mighty handy with your lasso. You roped that calf back there as slick as any top hand."

Bob grinned with pleasure. "I'm better than I used to be," he agreed, "but I still waste plenty of loops."

"Well, it's harder to rope when you're riding fast and when the animal you're after is running and dodging."

"I noticed that," Bob said. "And I can see I still need plenty of practice."

Once the cows and calves were in a group, it was not so difficult to drive them. They seemed willing to stay in a bunch, and all that was necessary was to keep them moving ahead and hold the occasional stragglers in line.

As they were riding homeward, driving the herd before them, Montana's sharp eye caught sight of something in the bushes. He called to Bob and told him to look. At first Bob could see nothing. Then he spied a tan object underneath a bush.

"Looks like it might be a 'dogie,' poor little fellow," said Montana, riding over toward it.

"A dogie!" Bob repeated, thinking Montana had mispronounced the word doggie. "It looks like a young calf to me."

"So it is," laughed the cowboy. "That's what a dogie is—an orphan calf. This little fellow looks so hungry that I'm afraid something has happened to its mama. But

117

we'll take a look around and find out. There's a mean bog hole hereabouts."

Calling to Shorty, whose job was to herd the cattle as they were rounded up, the foreman ordered, "Shorty, you keep the herd homebound."

Montana then rode toward a swampy bit of ground, reined his pony, and studied the scum that covered a bit of lowland. Finally he pointed to a place almost in the center.

"See that horn sticking up over there?" he asked Bob, who had followed him.

Bob nodded.

"I reckon that's where our dogie's mama is," the foreman said. "I reckon if we'd come along yesterday or the day before we'd have saved her. I've always wanted the boss to put a fence around this place. We lose a critter or two in here every spring. But later in the summer it's a good water hole—the only one on this part of the range."

They rode back to the little calf. She had not moved. Montana dismounted, picked her up, and put her in front of the saddle.

"What are you going to do with her?" Bob asked.

"Carry her home for you to take care of," the cowboy grinned. "It'll be another pet for you."

"That will be swell," Bob said.

It was dark when they reached the ranch house. Bob

slid from Peanuts so sore and stiff that he could hardly walk. He wanted nothing so much as to go right into the dining room and eat a huge meal and then to crawl into bed. But, remembering that a good cowboy always takes care of his horse before he attends to his own needs, he took the saddle off Peanuts, rubbed him down, put him in the stall, and fed him. Then he stumbled into the dining room and fell to with good will on the plate of stew that Cookie dished up for him.

Bob saw Montana come into the kitchen and go out again, but he was too tired and hungry to pay much attention. He was just finishing his meal when the cowboy came in and sat down at the table.

"Where have you been?" Bob asked.

"Feeding the little dogie," Montana said briefly. "Remember him? I thought he was supposed to be yours. But anyway the little critter was nearly starved. I got its tummy full before I came in to put on my own feed bag."

"Oh," said Bob faintly. Then he promised, "I'll take care of the dogie after this."

True to his word, the next morning Bob went out before he ate his breakfast and set about teaching the dogie calf to eat. Cookie helped him dilute a can of condensed milk in warm water and put it in a bucket. He pushed the dogie's nose into the milk, but nothing came of this but much puffing and snorting and violent struggling.

119

Then Bob tried dipping his fingers in the milk and letting the calf suck them. This worked better. But Bob was determined to teach the dogie to drink out of the bucket. He struggled for half an hour, then the calf finally got the idea and drank willingly.

Bob went in to find his breakfast cold, but he ate with the satisfaction of knowing that he had carried out the cowboy's first rule of caring for the needs of his animals before he cared for his own.

120

10. Circle K Branding

Bob had a vague idea of what a branding was. He had seen the Circle K brand on the cattle roaming the ranch. He had seen the collection of branding irons hanging in the ranch blacksmith shop, and he was filled with excitement over the activity ahead. He sensed the excitement of the men, too. Plainly a branding was one of the big events on the ranch.

So far Bob hadn't asked too many questions. He hated always to be going around asking about things and having the men laugh at him, as though his ignorance were too funny for words. By keeping his eyes and ears open he could pick up a lot of information. But there were some things about branding that he hadn't been able to pick up. Well, he would wait and see.

It was still early in the morning when the neighbors began to arrive.

"What are they doing here?" Bob asked. "Do they think this is a picnic or something?"

Shorty chuckled. "A branding is a sort of picnic," he explained. "The neighbors all come in to help. Even folks from town come—folks who have had some experience handling cattle. They get a kick out of it. And the women bring things to eat."

"What's Cookie doing over by that long hole in the ground?" Bob was forgetting his resolution not to ask questions.

"Don't you know?" Shorty asked. "That's the barbecue pit. Some of the men dug it yesterday while you were out on the roundup. Then they built a fire in it and threw in a lot of rocks. When they got red hot, Cookie had a whole beef put on top of them, and he covered it with his own special concoction of sauces and seasonings. Then the men piled leaves all over it and filled the pit up with dirt. The beef's been cooking in there all night."

"Is it done yet?" Bob asked eagerly.

"Cookie is nosing around to see if everything is going all right, but the dirt won't be taken away till the boys are ready to eat. Then," Shorty smacked his lips, "you will taste something the like of which you never tasted before. You'll never forget it as long as you live!"

Bob's mouth watered. "Golly!" he cried, turning from the pit to watch some of the neighbor women carrying delicious looking cakes, pies, and golden-brown loaves of bread into the kitchen. "I didn't know that branding was such fun!"

A commotion over in the round corral drew him there. He saw several bonfires in the center of the ring and on one side a cluster of mother cows and their calves huddled against the fence. Bob had figured out for himself why corrals were round—so that the cattle or horses would not get hurt from crowding into a corner.

As he clambered to the top pole to watch the proceedings, he was conscious of someone beside him.

"Howdy," Jerry greeted him in friendly fashion. "How do you like your first branding?"

"I feel sorry for the calves," Bob admitted. "It must hurt terribly."

"I don't believe it hurts too much," Jerry said. "It's all over so fast. Not half as bad as having your tonsils out. Besides, their hides are tough, and the iron doesn't burn clear through the skin."

Bob watched fascinated as the men thrust the branding irons with the Circle K mark into the bonfires; as Montana rode around the circle cutting out and roping the calves to be branded.

"Cowboys have to be pretty strong, don't they," Bob remarked to Jerry, "to be able to throw the calves on their sides that way."

123

Jerry nodded. "But it takes two of them to hold the calf down while someone slaps the iron on its hip."

While the calf was down, the men notched its ear and gave it a hypodermic injection against hoof-and-mouth disease. It was all over in a moment, and the calf leaped to its feet and ran to its mama bawling over the ill treatment it had received.

"I don't exactly see the sense of branding," Bob said.

"It's pretty necessary," Jerry explained. "The brand is the only way of telling who owns the animal."

"But folks have fences all around their ranches," Bob protested. "Everything on this spread belongs to my uncle. I should think anyone would know that."

"Yes, but sometimes animals break through fences and get onto someone else's property. Owners couldn't tell their own stock without a brand. And if they didn't brand their cattle, rustling would start again the way it used to be."

"I know what rustling is," said Bob, proud of his knowledge. "It's stealing cattle or horses."

"Exactly," said Uncle John, as he came up and leaned on the fence beside Bob. "It was branding that helped to do away with cattle rustling. Every cattle owner has to register his brand with the state office. And inspectors examine hides to see if there are any signs of a brand's having been worked over."

Branding the calves
with the Circle K mark

"Isn't there ever any cattle rustling any more?" Bob asked. He rather hoped sometime to see a real cattle rustler.

"Oh, yes—some," his uncle told him. "But it's pretty rare. You see, a number of years ago there weren't any fences in the cattle country. So of course herds of cattle got pretty well mixed up. It was then that men took to branding in order to recognize their own livestock."

"So you see," Jerry said, "there's sense to everything done on a cattle ranch."

Uncle John laughed. "That's right, Jerry," he agreed. Then handing Bob a long stick he said, "How would you like to keep tally for a while? Just cut a notch with your jackknife for each calf that gets branded."

Bob took the stick eagerly and settled himself on the top rail. Jerry sat beside him and helped keep count. The boys found it a fascinating show. Every calf acted differently. Some were quite clever in dodging the rope that was to draw them to the branding fire. But the men doing the roping were cleverer, and eventually each calf was led to its fate.

Some of the cowboys, Crowbait especially, did not always wait for the calf to be roped but would seize one and attempt to throw it without help.

"That's show-off stuff," Jerry remarked scornfully.

As fast as one group of calves was branded, they and

126

their mamas were turned out to pasture and another bawling group took their place.

Bob noticed that the branded calves started grazing as soon as they were turned out. "I guess you're right, Jerry," he admitted. "They do seem to forget their pain pretty quickly."

A little later he said, "I wish they would let me try roping and throwing a calf."

"Maybe they will," Jerry encouraged. Then he turned and said suddenly, "Say, how did our trick of mixing up the horses at the shindig work out here?"

"Not so good." Bob grinned ruefully. "It was Montana, not Crowbait, who woke up off the home range. I didn't want to play a joke like that on Montana, because he is sure a swell guy. He's even going to let me train a colt myself."

Jerry whistled his appreciation of this. "Montana *is* a swell guy," he agreed. "Too bad our trick caught him."

Bob saw Cookie bustling around the barbecue pit, and the thought of the buried roast made him hungry. He wished Cookie would do something about uncovering the beef, but plainly the men intended to work right through until the job was done. The sun had started on its downward path, but still they showed no sign of stopping. Bob sighed and tried to forget his hunger.

Later in the afternoon Montana rode up.

"Would you let me try to rope a calf and throw him?" Bob asked.

"Why not?" answered Montana reasonably. "Wait till this bunch is about half finished, then give Jerry your tally stick, and hop down into the corral. I reckon you'd better rope from that hoss over there by the gate. He's a good roper. And if you throw your calf without help I'll let you go to line camp with me."

Bob grinned his thanks.

"But you'd better pick a little one," Montana warned, "because you aren't the biggest man in the crew, you know."

A few moments later Bob mounted the horse that Montana had pointed out, then looked about to pick a calf he thought he could handle. As soon as he spotted it, he started twirling his rope. He wasted the first loop. He could see the men grinning as he hauled it in and started forming it again. He gritted his teeth and resolved that the next time he would place his loop. And he did. It sailed easily over the calf's neck, and the creature calmly walked right through it. Bob felt both foolish and angry as a roar of laughter greeted his second failure.

Red-faced, he formed his loop the third time. This time he placed it, and his horse held the line taut while the calf at the end of it leaped and bawled. Bob slid from the saddle and ran to the animal. Seizing one front and

128

one hind leg he tugged with might and main. He gave a mighty heave, and with a grunt the calf fell to its side. Bob looked up in triumph.

What he saw made his eyes freeze with terror. Charging toward him, head lowered, came the calf's mama. She was snorting angrily, and her short horns looked very vicious.

Suddenly a loop whizzed through the air. The cow skidded on her knees and tumbled at Bob's feet. A rope from Montana's hand had saved him!

Bob scrambled up to safety. From the fence rail he watched the other men finish off the calf he had thrown. After it was released, the furious mama walked over and licked her hurt baby.

"That was good work, kid," Montana called. "You did what you set out to do, even if you had to pick a calf with a mean mama!"

Bob smiled weakly. But he wished that everything he tried to do would not turn out to be a flop or in some way make him ridiculous.

"Yipee!" Jerry cried as the last calf was branded. "Now we can eat!"

He and Bob trudged along with the weary men to the wash bench to wash their hot, dusty faces and hands. Then they all hurried to the long table that had been set up under the trees. Women were bustling around, loading it with pies, cakes, baked ham, bowls of potato salad, baked beans, pickles, jam, jelly, and different kinds of bread and rolls.

"Oh," Bob cried at the sight of the food, "I'm starving! Why doesn't someone start to eat?"

Then the barbecue pit was opened, and the cooked beef was hauled up and laid on a clean tarpaulin.

Bob sniffed the delicious aroma that rose from it. He leaned against Jerry for support. "I'm going to die if I don't start eating," he said weakly.

"Me, too," said Jerry. "Let's get going."

Everyone had the same notion at the same time. The two boys joined the line of men who filed by the long table, each picking up a plate and piling it high with good things.

Cookie bent over the beef and sliced from it great savory hunks to place on slices of bread.

Each man, when he had heaped his plate until it could hold no more, would seek a shady place to eat. Some sat on the edge of the porch, but most of the cowboys squatted on their haunches with their plates balanced on their knees, the way they ate while on roundups.

Bob and Jerry glanced meaningfully at each other and grinned. Then, as if by prearranged plan, they took their heaped plates to a spot halfway between the table and the barbecue pit and sat themselves down on the ground.

"Convenient for refills!" laughed Jerry.

It was the most unusual and enjoyable picnic Bob had even been on. The barbecued beef was delicious. Twice he and Jerry went back for more, each time adding all of the extras their plates would hold.

"I may be sick when this is all over," Bob grunted to Jerry, "but I don't much care. This is the swellest food I ever tasted."

"They always have good food at brandings," Jerry told him. "But wait till you taste the food on the beef roundup. There aren't so many kinds as there are here, but that is really when grub tastes best."

"When is beef roundup?" Bob asked.

"At the end of the summer. Just before rodeo. You have the best part of ranch life to look forward to."

"I'm afraid I won't be here," Bob said regretfully. "School starts before then."

"Shucks!" Jerry cried. "That's a dickens of a way to do. School around here never starts until rodeo is over. It wouldn't be any use. The kids wouldn't go. You'd better get your dad to let you stay."

Bob shook his head. "No use," he said. Then added wistfully, "But I wish I could!"

11. The Lesson of the Rope

"WHEN will you be ready to commence breaking the colt?" Montana asked a few days after the branding.

"Right now!" Bob cried, his eyes shining with eagerness. He had been waiting for the foreman to find time to get him started on what seemed to him the most important project in the world.

"Of course, you've got a few things to learn first," Montana told him. "How to put a saddle on your hoss and get it tight enough, for instance." He chuckled at the memory of Peanuts' trick. "Not that you'll be able to use a saddle on the colt this year. He's not big enough. But any waddy worth his salt can use a rope and saddle a hoss right and all such things."

"That's just what I want to do," Bob cried.

Montana led the way to the fence rail and picked up one of the lightest stock saddles there. He threw it across

132

Peanuts' back and showed exactly how it should be done.

Bob had been keeping his eyes open. Right away he was able to adjust the bridle and saddle to Montana's satisfaction.

"You'll be a top hand yet," the cowboy said approvingly. "You've learned a lot since you found yourself under Peanuts' belly." He laughed again at the recollection. "But you still have plenty to learn. You'll have to be able to lasso the colt yourself and teach him the lesson of the rope before you can break him."

Bob's heart fell. He had hoped he was ready to commence breaking the colt immediately.

"You can't risk failing at the start," Montana told him. "And you must always be calm and sure of yourself, or the hoss will sense it and get spooky."

In a vague sort of way Bob already realized that before he could hope to control a high-spirited animal he must have learned to control himself. And that before he could hope to gain the animal's confidence he must have confidence in himself. He knew, even without Montana's telling him, how understanding horses were—how they seemed to sense nervousness or lack of self-confidence on the part of their rider.

"Now," Montana said, "we'll take a run out into the pasture and see how you make out roping a few calves from Peanuts' back."

133

For weeks Bob had been making life miserable for the animals near the ranch house, practicing his roping on them. Shep and Button ran now, whenever they saw him coming with rope in hand. And he was seldom without it. Button was so swift and clever at dodging that when Bob succeeded in roping the pet antelope he felt that he had really done something. Even the cowboys were likely to find themselves caught in his loop.

"Humph!" Crowbait, who did not enjoy being a target, had said. "Anyone can dab a rope on a man on foot. The thing is to rope from a moving hoss something that's moving, too."

Now Bob's moment had come to try his skill at this. Up and down and around he rode, practicing roping calves from a galloping horse.

For a while it seemed to him that he made no progress at all. He gritted his teeth and twirled the rope, determined that this time he would lasso the running calf, only to have the slippery creature neatly dodge the loop. It exasperated Bob until he was close to tears. At last he became so angry that he unwound the dallies that fastened his rope to the horn and, twisting the rope up into a tangled ball, threw it as hard as he could throw. At the same time he dug his heels into Peanuts' ribs. The pony, rightfully resenting this unfair treatment, bogged his head between his forelegs and neatly bucked Bob off.

134

As Bob sat on the ground, unhurt except for his dignity, Montana came riding up. He looked down at the furious boy. "I've been watching you," he said. "Get up. Pick up your rope and wind it, and climb back on Peanuts."

"I'll never learn to rope a moving animal," Bob choked. "And it makes me so mad to have 'em step right through my loop."

"I know that feeling well," Montana grinned. "We cowboys have that happen to us, too. But no real cowboy takes it out on his hoss, when he wastes a loop."

Bob's face turned red. He mounted Peanuts, wrapped a few dallies around the saddle horn and re-formed his rope.

"Sit your hoss easy now," Montana told him. "Roping is one of the things that you have to take easy at the same time you try hard at it."

Bob looked puzzled.

"It's kind of hard to explain," Montana said. "Of course you have to try, but the harder you try the worse you get."

Bob scratched his head in bewilderment.

Montana began again. "It's like this. You have to have all your senses alert and you have to try hard. But you must do it without tying your muscles up in knots. You've got to be sort of relaxed while you try. Get the idea?"

"I'm beginning to," Bob answered.

"Now watch me," Montana said.

He urged Silver to a gallop, cut out a calf from the herd, and started winding his rope arm while his intelligent horse pursued the swiftly moving yearling. He leaned forward in the saddle and half stood in the stirrups. Bob could see that while every sense was alert, the cowboy was still relaxed enough to allow his muscles to work almost automatically. His rope snaked out, and the calf went somersaulting over the grass. Montana jumped down and quickly loosened the rope. Then he lifted the calf in his strong arms, set it on its feet, and gave it an affectionate pat on the rump.

"See how it's done?" he grinned, climbing back on his horse.

"It sure looks easy when you do it," Bob said.

"I've been practicing for years," Montana reminded him. "By the time you're my age, if you keep up your practice you may be almost as good as I am!"

"I doubt it," Bob answered.

"Well, don't give up. Now loosen up. Stop gritting your teeth, and keep on trying. But if I ever catch you kicking your hoss again for something that's your fault, the deal about the colt is off."

Montana galloped away, and Bob began again. There was certainly a trick to it, he discovered. But at length success rewarded his efforts twice in succession. After a few more times he knew he had got the "feel" of it. Not every loop found its target, but he was becoming steadily more skillful. He felt the elation that comes with hard-won success.

For several days Bob kept up this practice. Then at last the great day came when Montana said, "How about it, partner? Do you feel ready to begin gentling the colt?"

Bob nodded his head. "I'm ready," he said with quiet confidence, although he was bursting with excitement.

It was a warm and golden day. The sky was a cloudless blue bowl. Bob drew in big lungfuls of the sage-scented breeze and felt happiness and power run through his veins like quicksilver.

Peanuts snorted and stretched his neck, asking for the rein. Bob glanced over at Montana. At a nod from the cowboy Bob loosened his pull on the lines and the two ponies went galloping over the prairie, their manes and tails waving. Bob's cheeks grew flushed and the swift air rushed through his hair.

When they reached the pasture where the dams and their colts were penned, Silver and Peanuts slowed down. Bob's heart thumped at the sight of the bay colt with the three white feet—the colt he was to gentle— racing up and down the length of the field, with flying mane and tail.

"Pretty sight," Montana drawled. "But before you start to gentle the colt, you ought to name him."

"I've done that already," Bob told the cowboy. "I've named him Boots. On account of his white legs. And because I want cowboy boots more than anything in the world—next to a horse," he confessed. "Boots just seems to fit him somehow."

Montana nodded understandingly. He leaned over and opened the gate. The horses and colts pricked up their ears and looked up from their grazing or playing to study the creatures invading their domain. A few horses that had been gentled came toward the gate. They had learned that men were often the bearers of good things —water and food and sometimes a treat of oats. But they approached warily.

"There's Boots over there by the fence." Bob pointed him out to Montana.

The cowboy nodded. "O.K.," he said. "Go after him."

Bob's heels scratched his pony's sides and he started off at a slow gallop. His rope arm was unlimbering, but sudden panic gripped him. What if he should fail?

"Whoa there! Whoa there!" he said to himself. He could not accomplish anything with his nerves tied up like this and his heart in his throat. He must recapture that feeling of confidence and power that had brought success. If he did not, the pony would sense his panic

138

and might, Bob knew, be spooky with him ever after.

So, instead of galloping straight for the herd, Bob rode to the end of the pasture. He drew in deep breaths, his eyes closed tight. Slowly the feeling that he wanted came to him—the sense of confidence and power. He turned Peanuts and galloped straight for the herd, his rope arm circling.

It took only a hint for Peanuts to sense which colt Bob was trying to cut out, and he worked beautifully as his rider headed between the dam and her frightened colt. The loop circled over Bob's head, snaked out, and settled around the colt's neck. Peanuts drew back in his tracks, taking up the slack in the rope. The colt whinnied and plunged, and the mother came galloping to his side.

"Oh, Boots!" Bob almost cried out. "I don't want to harm you. Please stop struggling! Let's be friends without my having to hurt you."

Montana rode up and whirled his rope, catching Boots around the rump. "Work him toward the west gate," he called to Bob.

Pulled from both ends, there was nothing for the little colt to do but allow himself to be dragged quickly to the gate and through into a smaller adjoining pasture. The distraught mother came, too, nuzzling her baby.

Montana loosened his rope and took the one Bob had. "I'll hold this," he said. "You climb down and try to get

139

close to Boots. Talk to him. Put your hands on him. Let him get used to you. Loosen the noose a little."

Bob followed Montana's instructions.

"There now, Boots, baby," he said soothingly. "Don't be afraid of me. We're going to be pals. I'll bring you sugar every day. You're going to learn to come when I whistle. I won't harm you. Please don't struggle. Let's get this bad part over fast."

The colt soon learned that struggling against the thing around his neck was painful. He stood still, trembling in every limb and leaning against his mother, who nickered and nuzzled comfortingly. Bob put his hands out and touched the silky neck, then his fingers loosened the noose again. At this hint of freedom the colt lunged once more, and the painful choking was repeated until Bob could get close enough to loosen the rope again.

"Oh, Boots, please don't!" Bob cried out. "I don't want you to be hurt. Can't you understand? And you needn't be, if you just won't struggle."

As Bob talked soothingly to Boots and rubbed the silky neck and nose, there swept through him a sense of happiness such as he had never known before. He already loved this colt.

"That's right," Montana said approvingly. "Keep talking and standing close. Let him get used to you. Your voice and your smell."

*Bob talked soothingly
to the colt*

After a time Montana told Bob to take off the noose and let the colt go. The moment the hated rope was off, the colt went galloping over the grass, his mother keeping between him and the enemy.

"That's enough for the first lesson," Montana said. "Now help me cut out about four other likely looking colts here. I'll halterbreak them this summer. They and their mamas will be company for Boots and his dam."

"Do you suppose that Boots has learned the lesson of the rope?" Bob asked.

"I reckon so," Montana nodded. "He acts like a right smart little critter. You may have to rope him the next time you try to catch him, but I don't believe he will fight the rope again. Just seeing you start to whirl it may be enough to make him stand still. If it isn't, tossing the rope across his neck ought to do the work."

After they had cut out four other colts and their dams and driven them into the smaller pasture, Bob and Montana galloped homeward.

"How do you halterbreak a colt?" Bob asked.

"I'll show you at the corral," Montana said. "There's a two-year-old filly there that's learned the rope lesson and is ready for the next grade."

Bob sat on the top pole of the corral and watched the filly receive her first lesson in being broken. Montana threw his rope so that it rested on the animal's neck. So well had the filly learned the lesson of the rope that she stood still. Then Montana stepped up and with a swift motion thrust the halter over her head and snapped the buckle.

This was something new, and the filly yanked back, sitting on her haunches like a large dog. Quickly Montana wound the rope around the snubbing post. He stood there, holding the rope end and waiting for the filly to tire of pulling with all her might.

Finally the surrender came. The pony gave a sudden lurch forward, releasing the strain on her neck. In an instant Montana was at her head, his hand on the halter close to the filly's mouth, his other hand stroking her neck. All the while he talked soothingly to her and walked back and forth in front, allowing his arm to brush her nose. Then he pulled off the halter and climbed up beside Bob.

"Is that all there is to it?" Bob asked.

"That's the first step," Montana drawled. "After you keep doing that all summer, you can call a colt halter-broken."

"Does that mean it's ready to ride?" Bob asked.

"The next summer it all has to be done over again," Montana admitted. "Only in about half the time. But this isn't all there is to it. After you get a colt so you can slip the halter on without a struggle, you get him used to

143

being led at different gaits. And he has to learn what 'whoa' and 'get up' mean. And you wave a blanket around. Put it on his back. Lean on his back. Things like that, so that when he is big enough to bear a saddle it isn't such a shock to him."

"Have all the horses you break been halterbroken?" Bob asked.

"I should say not," Montana laughed. "They're all broncs that have been allowed to get full-grown on the range, as free as the air. So when it comes time to break them, you really have a job on your hands."

"Wouldn't it be better," Bob asked, "to halterbreak them when they are young?"

Montana nodded. "When I have my own spread," he said dreamily, "I'm going to raise mostly fine hosses. And when I do, they're all going to be gentled like that. When they're colts. None of this breaking full-grown hosses on my ranch. It always takes something out of an animal to wear it down until it's forced to give in."

"I wouldn't want Boots to be trained that way," Bob agreed.

Every day now, after his chores were done, Bob rode to the west pasture and worked with the colt. The routine was always the same. First he would sit on the fence and whistle. But Boots' only response would be to run wild eyed to his mama. This performance made Bob feel hurt and dismayed. He had dreamed so long of having a pony that would nicker a welcome and come running in answer to his whistle! And Boots showed no promise of ever doing this.

For the first week Bob had to toss the rope over Boots' neck to get him to stand. Then it became possible to slip the halter on without a struggle. The first time this happened a joyous pride ran through Bob. He was making progress!

Then came the runs around the pasture, with Bob holding the halter strap and Boots kicking up his heels, thoroughly enjoying the game. Though to Bob's chagrin it was usually the colt who regulated the speed!

At the end of every lesson Bob reached in his pocket and drew out a lump of sugar and held it on his palm for the pony. Often now Boots would nuzzle him affectionately. And then Bob would put his arm over the animal's neck and rub the velvety nose, while the happiness that welled up within him over this companionship was so great that it almost hurt.

12. A Traveling Jackknife

"How would you like to spend a week at a line camp with me, partner?" Montana asked Bob one morning.

"Fine!" cried Bob. "If Uncle John will let me go."

"I asked him, and he's agreeable. I need help, and he says he can't spare any of the other men."

"Oh, swell!" Bob cried, his eyes sparkling. "Shall I pack my suitcase?"

"Whoever saw a cowpoke carrying a suitcase!" Montana scoffed. "We waddies always travel light. I don't believe old Peanuts would like a suitcase flapping against his side." He grinned at the idea. Then he told Bob, "We'll each take a roll of bedding. You can stick a change of clothes in yours in case we get wet."

Soon after breakfast the two of them set out toward the blue hills. Bob was mounted on Peanuts; Montana on Silver. Baldy was the pack horse.

Bob thought he had never been so proud and happy. He was the foreman's chosen partner, setting out to do important work on the range. The soft breeze brought a scent of sage. He drew in deep breaths, and the blood tingled through his veins. The squeak of saddle leather was music to his ears, and the rise and fall of the horse underneath him was the pleasantest feeling he had ever known. He could understand why a cowboy would never walk if he could possibly stay on horseback.

Montana threw him a companionable grin. "Kind of nice to be out riding the range, isn't it?"

Bob nodded happily. It was much more than "nice."

"I hate to ask such a dumb question," Bob finally said. "But what is a line camp?"

"It's a cabin out somewhere on the range," Montana told him. "Usually near a water hole where the livestock come to drink. The cowboys use it as a center to ride the range from. This spread is too big for us to cover it entirely and be back at the home cabin at night. Most big spreads have several line camps."

"Do men stay at the line camp all year?" Bob asked.

"Usually. Winter, when the weather is bad, is when the critters really need nursemaids."

"I can't see what there is to do at a line camp in summer."

"You'd be surprised," Montana replied. "A cowboy's

147

work is never done. When there isn't something like branding or a roundup or hossbreaking to tend to, we have to ride the range and look after the stock. We cattlemen get to know our livestock the way you know your school pals. We can tell when any strays get mixed up with ours. And of course we have to keep track that none of ours turn up missing. We have to see that fences are in repair and keep check on the cattle to see that they are growing and gaining weight. That's what counts in the fall, when the fat beef are marketed. "He looked straight at Bob. "Don't get the notion that a line camp is all a picnic or a nice, lazy vacation."

"I'm not afraid of work," Bob stated stoutly.

"You aren't lazy," Montana agreed. "Else I wouldn't have picked you to be my partner."

Bob's heart swelled with pride at his friend's use of the word partner.

At noon they stopped by a pleasant stream to rest— the horses, Montana explained, rather than themselves. They ate the sandwiches and pie that Cookie had wrapped up for them. Not since the branding had Bob known food to taste so good.

"I'd like to do this every day of my life," he declared.

Montana grinned indulgently. "It isn't bad," he agreed. He chewed on a tender stick of grass thoughtfully. "I've never known a cowboy who wanted to be anything else than just what he was—except that most of them hope someday to own their own spread instead of working for a boss."

He chewed awhile before he went on. "It isn't always too pleasant, though. In winter, when the blizzards howl and a fellow has to get out and try to keep the cattle on their feet, it isn't exactly a picnic. But I wouldn't choose any other life."

"I don't see why anyone would," Bob cried.

"Most people," Montana said thoughtfully, "want to be something else. Want to live somewhere else. But cowboys are contented. They like their work and wherever they are."

It was after dark when Montana and Bob reached the line camp. After taking care of the horses, they went into the cabin. There was a scurrying of tiny feet as Montana scratched a match. "Hate to disturb you mice and chipmunks," he said, "but we want to move in for a while."

Bob laughed, but he was glad of the light spread by the kerosene lamp in the center of the table.

"I don't mind the little fellows," Montana told Bob, "except that they're such untidy housekeepers."

A myriad of insects instantly began to swarm around the pool of warm light, many of them to their doom. In spite of the eerie shadows, Bob could see that the cabin consisted of only the one small room, with a built-in

149

*The savory smell
made Bob's nostrils twitch*

bunk covered with straw in one corner. Besides the crude wooden table with the lamp on it, there were a wooden bench and a rickety iron stove. A coffeepot sat on the stove, and a shelf back of it held a few pans and tin plates.

Montana whittled some kindling, put some wood in the stove, and touched a match. Soon the savory smell of frying bacon made Bob's nostrils twitch.

"How about peeling a few spuds for us?" Montana suggested.

Bob took out his jackknife. He had never peeled a potato in his life until he came to the Circle K, but now, thanks to Cookie's training, he was able to do an expert job. When he had finished, he placed the knife on the table and gave Montana the whole potatoes, which the cowboy deftly sliced into the hot grease left from frying the bacon.

While Bob stirred them, Montana opened a can of baked beans, then made coffee.

Bob sighed happily as he heaped his plate. Again he was sure that food had never smelled and tasted so good.

As soon as the supper things were cleaned up, Montana suggested that they "hit the hay."

Bob laughed as he looked at the bunk. For the first time in his life he could see the sense to the expression, except that the "hay" was straw. He helped Montana

151

loosen it up a bit and spread their blankets over it. Bob found it was not a bad bed, although he didn't stay awake very long to test its comfort.

Suddenly he sat bolt upright in the bunk, his hair prickling on his scalp. Reaching over, he shook Montana's shoulder. "What's that noise on the roof?" he whispered hoarsely.

"I don't hear anything," Montana said sleepily.

"Maybe it's mountain lions or cougars!" Bob was trying to keep his teeth from chattering.

"Well, they can't get in. Door's latched," the cowboy grunted. In a moment his heavy breathing told Bob that Montana was asleep again.

Slowly Bob relaxed and eased back under the blankets. If Montana wasn't worried, probably everything was all right. Anyway, the only sounds he could hear now were the soothing gurgle of the brook and the swish of the breeze in the pine trees.

Bob awakened to the fragrance of coffee and frying bacon. Montana was already up and had breakfast under way.

"Howdy, tenderfoot," he said teasingly as he glanced over to where Bob was sitting on the edge of the bunk, pulling on his socks.

"What do you mean, 'tenderfoot'?" Bob bristled. "Why, I'm practically a dyed-in-the-wool cowboy now."

"Not according to the way you dress, you aren't," Montana said scornfully.

"What's the difference between the way a cowboy and a tenderfoot dress?" Bob asked crossly.

"All the difference in the world," Montana told him. "A cowboy dresses from the top down. A tenderfoot dresses from the bottom up."

Bob, in the act of stepping into his overalls, looked up questioningly. "What do you mean, 'dresses from the top down'?"

"Well, it's like this," said Montana as he expertly flipped a pancake. "In summer cowboys sleep out in the open a lot. And in the winter the bunkhouse is cold as outdoors. Such being the case, the natural thing to do is keep as much of you covered up as you can while you're dressing. So a cowboy sits up in bed and puts on his shirt. Then his pants. Then his socks and boots. I've seen cowboys put on their hats first thing."

Bob laughed. He was splashing a little water from the basin daintily on his hands and face, feeling that at line camp he did not have to take the job of washing too seriously.

"Say, partner," Montana called, "my fire's kind of petering out on me. Would you shave off a little kindling?"

"What did you do with my knife?" Bob asked.

"Haven't seen it."

153

"But I put it right here on the table last night."

Montana shrugged. "I reckon you must have forgotten where you put it. It wasn't there when I set the table."

"But it was," Bob insisted. "I left it right there." He put his finger on the exact spot where he remembered placing it.

Montana put his hands on his hips and stared at Bob. "Do you by any chance happen to be doubting my word?"

Bob stared back angrily. He was positive that the knife had been on this exact spot last night. Montana must have moved it.

"Say, listen," he said slowly, "I know that cowboys are always playing jokes on each other, but I don't see anything funny about this. I need my knife. I can't cut kindling without it."

"I told you, I haven't seen your knife," Montana said.

"It's a very special knife," Bob went on. "It has four blades."

"I still haven't seen it," Montana said, and there was a look in his eyes that Bob had never seen before. "And I'm not in the habit of having anyone doubt my word."

Bob was angry, too. "Well, it couldn't walk off," he said stiffly.

"It might have at that," Montana answered sarcastically. "You said yourself it was a very special knife.

Maybe the four blades turned into legs and walked away."

He filled his own tin plate with flapjacks, bacon, and fried eggs. Bob did the same. Then they both sat, eating in silence. Bob had been famished when he first smelled the bacon, but now his appetite seemed to have fled.

Still in frigid silence they washed their dishes. Then Montana went outside, saddled Silver, and rode off.

Bob stood in the doorway, staring after the cowboy unbelievingly. So Montana was going off and leaving him here alone! He went outside to sit on a rock in the warm sun and brood upon his trouble.

The stream babbled happily. The silvery leaves of the quaking aspen danced and whispered. The air was filled with the clean scent of pine needles and moss. A magpie chattered noisily. A squirrel scolded from a near-by rock. A jack rabbit came bounding out from behind the cabin.

Bob sat there with his elbows on his knees and his chin in his hands, feeling lonely and abused. Suddenly he sat up straight, his eyes wide with surprise. A bushy-tailed animal with bluish-gray fur had darted from under the cabin. And in its mouth it carried something shiny—something that looked like a spoon.

Bob dashed after the little animal as it disappeared under a mound of sticks and rubbish piled against a rock. He picked up a stout stick and started digging, determined to investigate this queer home and to recover the spoon or whatever it was. The animal darted out the opposite side, as sticks flew right and left.

As the lair was laid low, Bob gasped. He stooped over and picked something up, blinking his eyes. It was his jackknife!

In the rough nest he had uncovered he also found two spoons, several round tops from syrup cans, a piece of glass, and numerous small stones and bits of metal.

Bob thrust the knife into his pocket and hurried to the shed. He saddled Peanuts more quickly than he had ever done before and climbed aboard. Then he set out at a gallop in the direction in which he had seen Montana head.

Since the foreman had taken his fence-mending tools, Bob followed the barbed wire. Before long he saw Montana. His rope was around a fence post, which Silver was pulling straight.

"Say, Montana!" Bob shouted as he rode up. "I found my knife. I'm sorry I—"

"Yeh?" the cowboy interrupted. "Where'd you find it?"

"It's the funniest thing. I saw an animal that looked a little like a squirrel run out from under the cabin with something in its mouth. I followed it and found a nest with a lot of junk in it. And my knife was there, too."

156

Montana nodded. "A pack rat," he said in a matter-of-fact tone. "I suspected it. But I was so put out at your doubting my word that I thought I'd let you find out for yourself."

"I've heard of pack rats," Bob said with a shamefaced grin, "but I didn't think of them this morning. They must have been what I heard on the roof last night, too."

"I reckon. They can make plenty of racket." Montana turned toward Bob. "Say, will you help me drive a bunch of cattle into a pasture? There's a sick cow among 'em. I've got her hobbled in a 'draw' over here so I can keep my eye on her in case she's got something contagious."

"Do cattle get contagious diseases?" Bob asked.

"Plenty of them. Hoof-and-mouth-disease, anthrax, distemper, tuberculosis. They have almost as many ailments as humans. That's why cowboys have to be nursemaids so much of the time."

Bob rode off happily beside his friend. The good, companionable feeling between them was established again. The cowboy had not said he was forgiven, but Bob knew.

The ailing cow in the draw seemed to be better. Bob helped give her a big dose of Epsom salts, which Montana claimed was a cure-all for most cattle illnesses. But Montana still considered it best to keep the herd from which she had come in the "isolation hospital," as he called the pasture in which he enclosed them.

That week at line camp proved to be one of the most enjoyable weeks of Bob's life. There were long, leisurely rides through the folds of the hills where deer and antelope stared at the human beings unafraid. Together, he and Montana saw to it that there were no breaks in the barbed wire, that the water holes were cleaned, that the herds were well and thriving. Now and then they found a late calf that had to be branded. And always there was the wonderful sense of comradeship between him and Montana. Bob hated to see the week come to an end.

13. Smoke!

"Whew!" puffed Montana as he and Bob, with Baldy following, rode back to the ranch house. He mopped his brow with his bandanna. "It hasn't rained since Noah. The grass is getting dry as tinder. And the water holes will all be drying up if this keeps on."

The grasshoppers rose in clouds as the horses jogged along through the dusty grass. Bob watched Montana anxiously study the sky for sign of a rain cloud. But only a few little wisps of cotton hung there, and they gave no indication of moisture.

"There's a nice breeze coming up," Bob said hopefully.

"It feels good," Montana admitted. "But it doesn't act as if it intended to stir up anything. Or—say! Does it?"

He stood up in his stirrups and stared off into the distance, shading his eyes with his hand.

Bob followed his example. "What are you looking at?" he asked curiously. "That little cloud of dust over there?"

"That's no cloud of dust," Montana gasped. "That's smoke!" With a quick turn, he threw Baldy's reins on the ground, then urged his pony forward.

Bob saw the cloud fan out slightly on the stiffening breeze and grow heavier. His heels pounded Peanuts' ribs, and he went galloping over the prairie behind the cowboy. When he saw Montana lean forward on his saddle, as though to help his mount to greater speed, Bob did the same.

"Should I ride back to the ranch and get help?" he shouted.

"No," Montana called back. "The men will see the smoke before you could get there. I need you here."

He was needed! A sudden surge of energy rose within him. In his zeal he gave Peanuts several unnecessary digs in the ribs.

Bob had no idea what they could do, just two of them alone against a prairie fire. He could see that it was in the direction of the pasture where Montana had penned the herd he was keeping under observation. A gully wound down the middle of that pasture. The fire would follow the natural draft caused by it.

Bob caught in his breath when he realized what might happen to the cattle if they should attempt to run before the wind-driven blaze. They would rush straight toward the barbed-wire fence at the end of the pasture! He wondered what Montana could do to save them.

He could smell the smoke now, as it rose in yellowish billowing clouds. Then he heard its moaning roar and felt the heat from the tongues of flame that licked at the edge of the cloud of smoke.

Everything fled before that blazing terror. Bob saw a group of antelope go bounding down wind; jack rabbits bounced past as if on springs; a coyote and several deer flew by like winged creatures. Birds fluttered frenziedly over the nests of fledglings they could not protect. Then came the fear-crazed cattle, thundering down the draw.

Montana and Bob urged their mounts on toward the terror from which all other animals were fleeing. The breath of the horses came in labored grunts, but they kept going forward.

Bob could scarcely breathe, the air was becoming so heavy. He did what he saw Montana do—drew his neckerchief up over his nose and put his head low against the pony's neck, turning it away from the direction of the fire.

The smoke was growing denser, and Bob could see the greedy tongues of flames licking at the precious grass. He noticed a pine tree in the path of the fire. It stood for a moment while the blaze swept by, then suddenly, like an explosion, burst into flames of red and blue.

From down the draw came the bawling of the cattle caught against the barbed wire. Bob's heels pounded mercilessly against Peanuts' sides, and the little pony spurted forward, following Silver's lead.

As they neared the fence, Bob could see Montana reach in his pocket for his wire cutters. Now he understood why a cowboy always carried them, and why Montana had asked him before they set out if he had his wire cutters with him. He took them out thankfully and galloped close beside Montana. As he reached the wire, again he did as he saw Montana do—leaned from his saddle and snipped the wires in front of him.

The zing of the tight wires as they were cut sounded like sweet music to them both. Through the gap in the wire poured the cattle, while Bob and Montana hazed them up the embankment.

Once the herd was headed in the right direction it needed no further guiding. Several of the animals were cut and bleeding from the cruel barbed wire. Singling out one of them, Montana raised his six-shooter and shot it through the head. Then he leaped from the saddle and with his big knife slit the animal down the middle. He tied his rope around a hind leg of the carcass and Bob's rope around another leg. Signalling Bob to follow, he galloped back toward the flames.

162

*They urged their horses
toward the blazing terror*

Bob quickly realized what was expected of him. He rode on the burned side of the blaze, Montana taking the other side, and between them they dragged the slit carcass along the line of fire. When the carcass was worn to shreds, Montana killed another injured steer and they repeated the performance. At last Montana turned to Bob and drawled, "Well, we've got it licked, I reckon."

At that moment the men from the Circle K came galloping up. Men from adjoining ranches came, too, for during a dry spell all ranchers were ever on the alert for that first telltale wisp of blue cloud that might bring tragedy to them all. They carried wet saddle blankets and wet cowhides.

Two more steers were killed to help in conquering the fire. When at last the blaze was out, a sickening strip of black was left over what had once been rich pasture grass.

Bob looked around at his comrades. Not one of them could he recognize. For the face of every one was as black as the strip of charred ground!

The men still rode back and forth, stamping out little patches that smoked or showed signs of flaring up again. But finally they decided it was safe to leave. Then the weary men turned their tired horses toward the cabin, the nearest place where good water was to be found.

Bob's eyes smarted as though some of the fire had got

into them, and his lungs felt burned out. He started to rush to the stream, to plunge his burning hands and face into its cool depths, but Montana held him back. The cowboy got out the lard pail, and each of the fire fighters reached in, took out a dab on his finger tips, and with it removed the first layer of smoke from his hands and face. Shorty's face was blistered from the heat. Crowbait had lost eyebrows and patches of hair.

After they were cleaned up enough to be recognizable, Montana said to Bob, "Well, partner, I reckon we've earned a bath and some clean clothes. We'll go back and pick up Baldy where we left him and drift for the home range."

"O.K.," said Bob. He wouldn't want to have to fight a prairie fire every day, but it certainly had been an adventure.

14. Down Lost Cabin Canyon

Bob sat on the fence top, staring disconsolately into the distance. Life on the ranch seemed dull after the excitement of the line camp and the fire. It was sultry hot. There was an uncomfortable, oppressive feeling in the atmosphere. The blue hills swam in a silvery haze. Birds whirled in the sky and colts kicked up their heels in the meadows. Bob's spirits were low. He had wanted to go horseback riding, but the men had needed the horses. Then Cookie had given him a mountain of potatoes to peel and had kept him hauling water and wood until dinnertime.

Suddenly Bob realized that Montana was leaning on the fence, staring at him and grinning. "A penny for your thoughts," came the drawling voice. "Only I doubt if they're worth it. Seems to me you're pretty much in the habit of daydreaming, young man."

"Well," Bob pouted, "there's nothing to do but chores."

Montana shrugged. "I reckon there's plenty to do for a body that's willing to get out and look."

"There is for you," Bob cried. "But what about me? Even Shep over there is more important on the Circle K than I am."

"I see your point," Montana said. "You hanker to feel important. That's natural. You also want a hoss under you. That's natural, too. But I reckon you aren't helping matters any by sitting there feeling sorry for yourself and letting your rope dangle like a piece of string."

"But what good does it do for me to keep practicing?" Bob blurted. "I'll never get a chance to rope cattle."

Montana chewed thoughtfully on a spear of grass. "I've found that anything I worked at hard always came in handy sometime, in some way or other," he said.

"I don't see what good learning to rope well will do anyone who isn't a cowboy."

Montana straightened up. "Have it your own way," he said indifferently. "If you want to sit on a fence and feel sorry for yourself, it's O.K. by me. But all the cowboys I ever knew *did* things instead of just dreaming about them." As he sauntered away he turned back to say, "You had got yourself to where you were pretty good with the rope. But you won't stay that way unless you practice every day. And you could spend a lot more time halter-breaking Boots, too. You've been kind of neglecting him."

Bob flushed at this. It was true. In spite of his affection for Boots, the job had been getting a bit monotonous.

"I'll go right over and give him his workout," he promised the foreman.

Montana looked up at the sky and nodded toward Laramie Peak, which was almost hidden by a dark cloud.

"Better get at it pronto then," he advised. He grabbed his hat as a gust of wind threatened to carry it away. "Beats all—this weather. Here this morning it was warm and peaceful and now it's blowing up another of those freak storms. Hampering our work every afternoon lately," he grumbled as he strode off toward the barn.

On his way to the colt pasture, Bob paused to feed Molly her daily lump of sugar. Old Molly had once been one of the top cow ponies of the Circle K. Now she had been retired as bell mare to keep the cavy together. She met him at the fence of the cow-pony pasture, nickering, and nuzzled his arm affectionately.

When he got to the training pasture, Bob climbed to the top of the gate and swung his legs over. Then he went through the daily routine of giving a sort of bob-white whistle to Boots. The pony had learned to recognize the whistle now and would perk his ears and look in Bob's direction.

Today Boots was chasing another colt around and around. He would nip at the colt, then the two of them would face each other and spar with their front hoofs. At Bob's whistle, Boots dropped to his four feet and looked toward him. Bob whistled again.

Then came the miracle for which Bob had been hoping for weeks. Boots came prancing toward him!

Bob slid down from the gate and held out his palm. As Boots licked the lump of sugar on it, Bob slipped his arm about the colt's neck and hugged him tight. "Oh, you did it!" he cried. "You did it! You came to my whistle! That makes you my pony no matter who owns you. You belong to me, because you came to my whistle!"

But Boots was rather skittish today. He dragged Bob along, hanging to the halter, then kicked up his heels and nipped him mischievously.

"Now, listen," Bob cried, yanking determinedly on the rope. "I'm boss around here. See? You're being naughty and a show-off and you won't get the rest of the sugar I brought until you behave."

As though he understood, Boots suddenly abandoned his skittish ways.

"That's better!" Bob gave him a pat. "Now you can have it."

He fed the colt the remaining lumps of sugar that Boots had been nuzzling his pockets for. Then he stood and watched as the white-footed colt trotted off to join his friends.

Bob sighed as he clambered over the gate. What was there to do now? He dismissed the thought of going back to the ranch house and writing a letter home. He could do that later in the day.

He stared at the sky. It was heavily overcast and the cloud that hung low over the hills was almost black. But the cloudiness was bringing a coolness which was a blessed relief from the heat of the past week.

At last Bob bestirred himself. Why not take a hike— a real one? For a long time he had wanted to explore Lost Cabin Canyon. This was a made-to-order day for such an excursion.

He went to the kitchen and filled his pockets with cookies. He looked about for his uncle or Cookie to leave word where he was going, but no one was around. His uncle had not forbidden him to walk over the ranch, and Bob was familiar enough with it now not to get lost again.

He started out, taking long strides and swinging his rope. He did this whenever he went anywhere, since Montana had told him that was the way cowboys became expert ropers.

As he walked along, he thought of the story of Lost Cabin Canyon. Gee, it would be great to be the one to

170

find the lost cabin and the gold mine! Even if others didn't believe the story, he did.

The canyon floor was rocky, and the walking was rather difficult. He could tell from the dead leaves and sticks on the rocks that sometimes water dashed over them, but now the stream bed was dry. After an hour's hard climb, he came to a place where the creek bed rather flattened out. Here he was able to clamber up to one side, where the going was somewhat easier.

He glanced at the sky and exclaimed aloud. The dark cloud he had noticed earlier in the afternoon had become almost black; it seemed fairly to touch the earth. The air had suddenly become quite cold. The wind came in fierce gusts. And there was a strange roaring noise back in the hills.

Bob looked around a bit uncertainly. Should he turn back or should he go on? A jagged streak of lightning split the sky and a peal of thunder rolled through the hills like a burst of artillery. He started back. Then the mystery of Lost Cabin Mine pulled him onward. It would be foolish to go back after coming this far. Perhaps the next turn would bring him to the broad gully that branched off toward Lost Cabin Canyon. He felt sure he would be luckier than the other treasure seekers had been.

Drops of rain as big as quarters pelted his face, but he

A jagged streak of lightning split the sky

kept on going. He didn't especially like the lightning that almost blinded him, nor the deafening rolls of thunder. But any moment now he might come to that broad gulch that would lead him to the cabin. He could take shelter there until the storm passed. Then he would find that wonderful mine.

The rain was beating down harder now. Bob bowed his head against it and kept on. Then he saw the gulch. There was no mistaking its V shape. Rather wide and shallow where it joined the rocky canyon, then growing narrower as it went back into the hills. A good thing his head was bent, he thought, or he might have missed it completely, overgrown as it was with shrubbery.

He scrambled down and crossed the canyon, clambering up on the other side. He would follow this bank, exploring all the likely places for the cabin to be. Then he would come back on the opposite side.

The going here was fairly easy, as the dense shrubbery had thinned out. The gulch was sheer and deep, but that did not interest Bob. The cabin would not be down there. It would be somewhere along the edge. Probably beside a stream. It might be a good idea to follow each stream he came to back for a little distance.

But what was that roaring noise? It was too steady a sound for thunder. As he listened, the noise grew in intensity and the atmosphere became awesome and strange. And now the roaring sounded terrifyingly loud.

Bob stopped in his tracks and his eyes widened. He blinked, then blinked again. He could not believe that he was actually seeing what he saw—a solid wall of yellowish, glassy looking water laden with debris, rushing down the gulch. Then he heard the clatter of horse's hoofs and, farther down the gulch, he saw the most incredible sight of all. A girl on horseback, galloping over the rocky gully bottom, trying desperately to outrace the oncoming wall of water!

At first Bob was too amazed to do anything but stand

in frozen horror. Then his mind began to act, even though his body would not. He must do something! But what?

The sides of the gulch were too steep for the girl to ride up. The wall of water was gaining on her.

His rope! As he thought of it, Bob's muscles came to life. He turned and raced along the edge of the gulch, rope in hand, ready. And then! He wanted to close his eyes to shut out the terror, but he stared, unbelieving. The water had overtaken the girl and she and her horse had disappeared beneath it. On its surface were whirlpools of dirty foam, uprooted trees and bushes. But no living thing was in sight.

It was so unbelievable it seemed like a nightmare. A sharp cry rose to Bob's lips. Then his heart caught up in a wave of relief as he saw the horse's head appear above the surface of the water. But where was the girl? His heart sank, then beat again as he saw her in the oily looking water, clinging to a good-sized branch. For a dizzy moment the branch with its burden spun around in a whirlpool. Then it was swept downstream. Bob ran, trying to keep up, but the water rushed faster than he could run.

At last the branch lodged against an overhanging tree, swaying dangerously. For a moment, while the tree held, the girl was safe. But at any time the force of the water

174

might tear out the already loosened roots and send the tree and its burden rushing down with the terrific current.

Bob yelled with all his might, trying to send his voice above the giant roar to the girl, clinging there so desperately. Again he shouted. This time his voice reached her and she looked up. Bob could see an expression of relief and hope appear on her frightened face.

Suddenly a wave of terrible realization came over him. That girl was depending upon *him* to save her life. There was no other help for her on earth. The tree against which she had been swept swayed more perilously every moment. It could not hold much longer.

Bob knew what he must do. His rope was in his hand. But panic swept through him. Had he forgotten how to use the rope? Were his arm muscles paralyzed?

The girl waved one arm weakly and Bob could see her mouth moving. He could not hear her words above the noise, but he had no doubt she was calling to him to save her.

He closed his eyes for a moment. Then, suddenly and almost without his thinking, the knowledge of how to use the rope came back to him and his muscles responded smoothly. The loop sailed out over the raging flood. Then fell, weak and futile, into the water.

Bob felt a terrific yank from the power of the flood.

175

He realized that if he had caught the girl he would have been pulled into the water. He must anchor his rope. Quickly he wrapped the bare end around a stout tree and re-formed his loop.

Again the brave lasso flew out, beautiful and true. This time the loop settled down over the girl's shoulders. In a second she had slipped the noose under her arms and grasped the rope with both hands. She looked up. Bob gave an encouraging nod and signalled for her to let go the tree. Then he braced his two feet against a rock and gripped the rope with both hands. The girl closed her eyes and slid into the boiling waters, trusting her life to the strength of her rescuer.

Bob pulled until it seemed as if his arms would be yanked from their sockets. He gritted his teeth until his jaws ached—and kept on pulling. He pulled until it seemed as if he could not endure the terrific strain another second. But still he pulled.

Finally the strain eased. Wrapping the slack of the rope around the rock and still keeping it taut, Bob ventured to the edge of the canyon and peered over. The girl lay on the bank below, face down, her feet still in the water.

Bob's heart leaped into his throat. Had she drowned while he was pulling her across the stream? He scrambled down the bank and turned her over. She was breath-

The lasso flew out
and settled over the girl

ing, but her eyes were closed and her lips were blue. Bob wondered if he should try artificial respiration. He made an effort to remember his Boy Scout training. Then the girl opened her eyes and smiled. A weak little smile.

Relief flooded Bob's heart. She was all right, then— probably only exhausted from shock and fright. He tried to drag her farther up on the bank, in case the water should rise. The girl attempted to help, but she still lay face down, her breath coming in labored gasps. Bob could see that this slender girl in the water-soaked jodhpurs was about his own age. But he felt much older.

"Hey," he said, touching her on the shoulder, "this won't do! You're soaking wet and cold. You'd better try to move around a bit."

The girl rose slowly to her feet and staggered along a few paces. "I'm so cold," she whispered between chattering teeth. "And my feet don't work very well."

At a sound from the bank above, Bob turned and looked up. "Well, I'll be jiggered!" he cried joyfully. "If there isn't your horse! He must have managed to keep his head up till he reached a place where he could scramble ashore."

"Good old Skylark!" the girl said shakily. Then she sank to the ground, covered her face with her hands, and burst into tears.

178

Bob looked at her in bewilderment. Girls were beyond him! Why on earth was she crying now that she was safe—and her horse, too?

"Say, listen!" he said with a shade of impatience. "You'd better save your crying till you get home."

"B-but—I can't help crying," she sobbed.

Bob looked down at her in disgust. After all her pluck —first clinging to the swaying branch, then letting herself be dragged across that torrent—to be crying now like a baby! He kicked at a root, trying to think what he should do to make her stop.

Reaching down, he yanked her arm and said crossly, "Come on, now. Let's get going. You might catch pneumonia if you don't get dry pretty soon. I'll help you aboard your horse and go along with you to wherever you live."

Somewhat to Bob's surprise, the girl let him lead her to the horse and help her into the saddle.

Bob took the bridle, intending to walk beside the horse.

"Climb up," the girl invited. "This horse often carries double." She smiled faintly. "Sorry I was so silly," she said as Bob led the horse to a rock and got up behind her. "You were wonderful to rescue me the way you did."

"What's your name?" Bob asked gruffly, embarrassed by her praise. "And where do you live?"

179

"I'm Rosemary Martin—one of the dudines at the Flying V Ranch. I remember seeing you there at the shindig last month. Which ranch are you from?"

Bob told her, then asked how she happened to be in the canyon alone.

"We all went on a picnic today," Rosemary said. "After we ate, one of the guides took us on a nature hike. I thought it was dull. So I climbed aboard Skylark and went in search of excitement."

"Well, I reckon you found it all right," Bob said shortly.

"I reckon I did," she agreed seriously.

The horse went along at a lively pace. It had stopped raining, but Bob was nearly as drenched as Rosemary and shivering with cold.

At the outskirts of the Flying V Ranch they met a group of horsemen. One man jumped to the ground and, running over to Skylark, pulled Rosemary from the saddle and hugged her until she begged for mercy. "Thank heaven you are safe!" he repeated again and again.

"I wouldn't have been, Dad," she said, "if it hadn't been for this boy here. He saved my life." And as the men gathered around, she told about the rescue.

Bob found himself being praised and patted on the back and having his hand shaken until he wanted to sink into the ground.

"I've got to be drifting back to the Circle K," he said abruptly. And his teeth chattered.

"Do you think for one minute that I would let you walk home?" Mr. Martin protested. "You're coming to the Flying V first. We'll get you dry and warm, then we'll take you home."

At the Flying V ranch house dry clothes were found for Bob, and he and Rosemary were wrapped in blankets and propped up in easy chairs before a roaring fire.

When Rosemary learned that this was Bob's first summer on a ranch, her eyes widened. "I thought you were a real cowboy," she said. "You certainly acted like one."

"Nope," Bob admitted, "I want to be someday. But now I'm just a tenderfoot. Like you."

"Then where on earth did you learn to rope?"

"I've been practicing a lot. Montana—that's our foreman—says that learning to rope is the first step toward being a cowboy."

"I must say that you've done all right!" There was genuine admiration in Rosemary's father's voice.

Bob squirmed again. "I'm quite warm now, sir," he said. "I really must be getting back to the ranch."

"I'll take you over in my car," Mr. Martin insisted.

Bob rolled his damp clothes into a bundle, said good-by to Rosemary, and started off with Mr. Martin.

Bob wanted to get out before they came to the ranch

house and try to reach his room unnoticed, but Mr. Martin would not listen to such a thing. Bob sighed. Now he supposed that there would be no way of hiding his latest adventure. Probably after this his uncle would keep him penned up in the barnyard.

There was a worried look on John Benton's face when he saw Bob and the tall stranger coming into the house. He looked at his nephew inquiringly, but before Bob could begin his explanation Mr. Martin was telling in glowing terms of Rosemary's rescue. Bob's face burned.

John Benton shook his head hopelessly. "Bob! Bob!" he groaned. "If my hair wasn't already gray, you would turn it that way!" But there was a new look in his eyes that made Bob's heart glad.

"Of course I am proud of my nephew," he told Mr. Martin. "It was a brave thing he did. But I'm responsible for his welfare, and I find the responsibility quite a worry."

"If I were you—" Mr. Martin looked at Bob with a twinkle in his eye—"I wouldn't worry about him. He impresses me as a boy who will be quite able to take care of himself. I wish I had a son like him."

Bob gave him a grateful look.

While Bob went up to change his clothes, his uncle took Mr. Martin out to his car. From his window Bob could see Montana join them and the three of them talking earnestly together. He did hope Montana would approve of what he had done.

A little later Bob went out and stood by the corral rail. Montana came up and leaned on the fence beside him.

"I reckon you were glad today that you knew how to use a rope. Eh, cowboy?"

Bob nodded and grinned up happily. He knew what the foreman meant. Montana wouldn't embarrass him by elaborate praise. But Montana had called him "cowboy"—something he had never done before.

"I wanted to find the gold mine," Bob said. "But I guess this was better."

"I reckon it was," Montana said quietly. He paused a moment, then went on, "Wandering along dry creek beds is bad business when it's storming back in the mountains. A cloudburst is always likely to bring one of those gully washers down some natural channel."

Montana went on talking, but the word "cowboy" was ringing in Bob's ears. Montana had called him "cowboy!" Bob had not been so happy in months.

183

15. Cowboy Fixin's

THE remaining two weeks Bob spent on the ranch zipped by like flipped pages in a book. He tried to prolong every one of the precious days by getting up earlier in the morning and by crowding as much activity as possible into its twenty-four hours. He even did his chores with a willingness that amazed Cookie. But at last the time came when he must leave the Circle K.

"How would you like to help the men drive a herd of beef cattle to the railroad?" Uncle John asked as Bob packed his suitcase.

"How would I like it?" Bob straightened up and stared at his uncle, scarcely able to believe his ears. "You mean you want me to *help?*"

"I mean just that," his uncle said. He placed his hand on his nephew's shoulder. "You've proved yourself a real cowboy. You have the makings of a top hand. Montana says so, and I agree with him. And the boys really need your help in driving the beef herd to town."

Bob's eyes sparkled. "If you want to come back to the Circle K next summer," his uncle went on, "there'll be a welcome waiting for you. And a pony of your own to ride. I've bought Montana's half of Boots, so I can give you a whole pony."

Bob reached over and seized the bedpost to steady himself. "You mean Boots will be—my—my—very own?" he gasped.

"I mean exactly that," said his uncle firmly. "Now finish your packing, so that your suitcase can be sent to town in the pickup."

"Hey, Bob!" Montana's voice boomed through the ranch house. "The mailman just brought a package for you."

Bob went racing into the living room. He stared in open-eyed amazement at the large box on the table.

"It must be a present from my folks," he cried. "But that's funny, because they know I'm coming home." He looked at the postmark. "It's from some place in California. I don't know anyone in California."

"Maybe if you'd open the box, you'd find out more about it," Montana suggested.

Bob tore the wrappings off the large box, scarcely noticing that his uncle and Cookie and the other men had come in and were standing around the room, watching him.

He stared and gasped and stared and gasped again. For in the box lay the finest cowboy outfit he had ever seen—California pants, tan leather chaps trimmed with huge silver conchas, a red silk shirt, a fine Stetson ten-gallon hat, and, best of all, leather boots with fancy white stitching.

Bob picked the things up, one by one, and examined them. "They look as if they would just about fit me," he said at last in a bewildered way.

The men laughed loudly at this remark.

"Maybe if you read what's in that envelope you left in the box," Montana drawled, "you'll find what it's all about."

Bob picked up the envelope and drew out a card.

"To BOB BENTON," he read slowly, "a mighty fine cowboy, in appreciation for saving Rosemary's life—TOM MARTIN."

Bob's knees suddenly became too weak to hold his weight. He sank into a chair. "Then—then—these things are really mine?" he stammered. "Maybe somebody had better pinch me!"

"I reckon you're awake all right," Montana laughed. "And you're a sure-enough cowboy now, with all the fixin's." He grinned as Bob picked up the boots and held them close. "Only a real cowboy would rate such fine, fancy-trimmed cowboy boots as those!"

"And when you come back next summer," John Benton added, "Boots will be big enough for you to ride."

Bob looked around at the circle of smiling faces and tried to blink away the mist in his eyes.

"Boots to wear and Boots to ride—" His voice trailed off huskily. There just weren't any words to express the happiness that flooded his heart.

Cowboy Words

Cowboys have a language all their own. You will find in this story a number of words used only in the cattle country. Since some of them may be unfamiliar to you, their meaning is given here.

bedsprings, full of—said of a lively bucking horse

bog his head—said of a horse that puts his head between his forelegs, getting ready to buck

bronco—an untamed horse

broncobuster—a man who makes a business of breaking horses

bunkhouse—a building for the cowhands on a ranch to sleep in

cavy—a band of saddle horses

chaps—leather seatless overalls to protect a rider's legs

chuck—food

conchas—shell-shaped metal disks used as trimming

corral—an enclosure for penning livestock

cowpuncher⎫—a cowboy; from the pointed pole used to prod
cowpoke ⎬   cattle into stock cars

crowhop—a bucking term

dally—a half-hitch with the rope around the saddle horn

draw—a shallow gully

dude wrangler—a man who "rides herd" on tenderfoot paying ranch guests

haze—to drive slowly

high-roll—a bucking motion in which the horse leaps high into the air

high-tail—to ride away fast

hombre—man

jackknife—a bucking motion in which the horse hits his front and back legs together

line-rider—a man who rides the range looking out for the welfare of his employer's stock and property

loco—crazy; with livestock this condition is a result of eating the poisonous locoweed

pickup—a small truck for hauling

pronto—in a hurry; right away

ranny—a top hand; a very good cowboy

roustabout—a man or boy who does odd jobs around a ranch

shindig—a cowboy dance

snubbing post—a stout timber, about five feet high, to wrap the rope around; it is set firmly in the center of the corral

spooky—nervous

spread—a ranch including the buildings, livestock, and employees

sunfish—a bucking term describing a twisting motion

swap ends—a bucking term describing a half-circle turn in the air

189

tenderfoot — one unused to western ways

top hand — a superior cowboy

waddy — a cowboy

weaver — a bucking horse with a weaving motion

wrangler — a herder of saddle horses

wrinkle his spine — a bucking term

COWBOY SADDLE

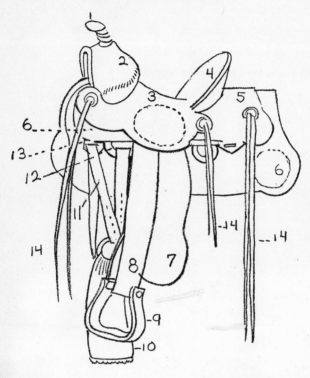

1	horn	8	stirrup leather
2	fork	9	stirrup
3	seat	10	cinch
4	cantle	11	latigo
5	back jockey	12	riding ring
6	skirt	13	latigo holder
7	fender	14	tie strings